Hell and the High S

When retired US marshal John Durant goes in search of his friend Lucas Gray, he finds nothing but lies and simmering tensions. A dubious sheriff, two drunkard woodcutters and a group of ranch hands all share the same sinister secret.

Fed the same official line, Durant won't be deterred. Aside from his growing feelings for Anne Slocum, his determination to learn the truth of Lucas's disappearance keeps the ex-marshal in the dying settlement of Cooper's Town. Soon, dying is the operative word. Hell breaks loose and war breaks out, as desperate men strive to hide their crimes. Durant sees very clearly that his battle for justice and truth lies through gun smoke and mayhem. He must go to Hell and the High S!

Hell and the High S

Clay Starmer

A Black Horse Western

ROBERT HALE · LONDON

ISBN 978-0-7090-9269-8

Robert Hale Limited
Clerkenwell House
Clerkenwell Green
London EC1R 0HT

www.halebooks.com

Typeset by
Derek Doyle & Associates, Shaw Heath
Printed and bound in Great Britain by
CPI Antony Rowe, Chippenham and Eastbourne

CHAPTER ONE

He rode with thoughts as dark as those distant black, massed hills. A host of possibilities he'd considered then dismissed – most unlikely given the man he sought. Finally, blanking his mind, he let his mustang pick its own pace across a vast grass landscape baking beneath the fiercest fire-faced sun.

At length, John Durant – six-foot of hardened ex-US marshal – halted the stallion at a creek's edge. He unlooped a canteen from the saddle horn and swallowed its tepid contents, trying to ignore the worry that gnawed at his guts. He shook his head, retied the canteen's strap then dived to the ground as a gun blast shattered the day's sweltering quiet.

He had the leathers to hand fast – making for a clump of cottonwood. Inside there he'd have half a chance.

He ran for his life, shrieking slugs pursuing his quickening steps. Whilst most flew harmlessly by, one whipped worryingly close to his head and another ripped into the parched underlay of flaked-dry soil.

Mercifully, though, he reached the trees unscathed and dragged the horse in. In no time, he'd got the stallion's reins lashed to a branch and a carbine in his grip. Now he'd fight back. He settled on a firing position – a site between two close-set trees – but lurched back with a curse. A slug crashed a passage through overhead leaves whilst another slammed into a gnarled trunk with a kickback of splintering bark.

Durant spat and scanned the distance. An uplift of dust signified something moving in fast and he soon defined the shooters: two men clad in denim and dark hats and both astride quarter horses. They closed at a gallop, their rifle fire shredding the space about the cottonwoods.

'Hell's teeth,' Durant growled. 'I've got no choice.'

Suddenly it happened: all his held-down rage surged to the fore. He'd slaughter these assailants to seek some assuage from that pent-up grief since losing his wife a year earlier.

He levelled the carbine, his finger teasing at the trigger. Yet, clearer reasoning got to him. He shook his head, inched the rifle's muzzle slightly to the side. The weapon barked in his hands then, and an instant after one of the riders spun off his horse with a pained howl.

The second rider moved fast. With his horse stilled, he leapt from the saddle and knelt beside the fallen other. Almost instantly, though, he inched to his feet again, yelling at the copse, 'You mean that shot, mister?'

'Yeah,' shouted Durant. 'He'll sting a bit.'

Even as Durant's gravelled voice subsided, the injured man sat up with his right arm swathed in blood.

'Now,' Durant roared on. 'You fools loose any more bullets my way, so help me, I'll plant my next slugs between your goddamn eyes.'

The warning worked. Both stayed put, the wounded one's countenance reflecting intense pain, the other man's look a mixture of anger and suspicion.

At length, the latter, a black-haired six-footer shouted, 'Mister, walk out slow, gun down and hands touching sky! There're twenty fellers following and you're in a heck of trouble.'

Durant pondered a moment but guessed it was a ruse. 'It might be,' he drawled. 'But you'll be dead before they get here.'

The black-hair shrugged before lodging his rifle back on the saddle. 'You've got the winning hand in them trees.' He glared at the thicket. 'Come out, mister. Steve can't shoot and I won't.'

Durant untethered his horse and when he stepped into view, he had his Colt .45 to hand.

'Just in case,' he drawled.

The injured man, back on his feet, struggled into the saddle with a groan of agony. Once astride his mount, he glared furiously and snapped, 'Get off this land fast, mister. Next time you'll be the one doing the bleeding.'

Durant shrugged. 'I don't know hereabouts,' he offered. 'I saw branded cattle, right enough. I guess they're yours?'

The injured one, a freckled, fresh-faced character had a fringe of blond hair and striking blue eyes that flashed as he spat, 'That's right, feller. There're markers enough about my land and you've passed plenty without heeding their words.'

Durant shrugged. He'd seen a host of signs advising trespassers to keep out. Yet, he'd had no choice. He'd followed Luke's directions exactly and that took him past those notices.

Subduing his bubbling rage, Durant pinned the man called Steve with a piercing look as he muttered, 'Summat's not right. My friend farmed yonder and now his place is deserted; your cattle are in his fields.'

What Durant had found at Green Ash Farm had left him shocked: a dilapidated log house stood against a backdrop of encroaching creosote and unthinned trees. The building just decayed in the inevitable way of abandonment: gaps left to widen, dirt obscuring windows, and vines, from their stranglehold on the roof, pursuing a destructive passage into everything.

Inside, through the open door, wind-carried detritus had settled thick – tumbleweed lodged at the back wall, moulding leaves and dust enough to bear a host of critter marks.

The yard had fared no better. Most of the corral's fence rails hung at angles off tilting posts; a gallows gate had collapsed and a pigpen stood as a space of vacated hutches, its plank surround flung and rotting a distance away. Near the farmhouse, a pile of uncovered timber gradually deteriorated.

Yet, the pastures heaved with cattle – longhorn grazing contentedly in those lush, flatland fields. Most rested in well-fed lethargy and all possessed an S brand seared to the flank.

Frowning as he'd taken a last glance back at that wreck of a dream, Durant had re-read Luke Gray's letter:

John, I've arrived. Have bought most beautiful farm and so cheap. It's called Green Ash and is six miles due north of Cooper's Town. I haven't been there yet but will when need supplies. I'll have goats, pigs etc and a peaceful life till I die. Please visit anytime. Luke.

An anguished shout brought Durant out of his sombre musings. The young man called Steve winced and tried to flex his blood-soaked arm. 'Mister, you got it all wrong. I've got *my* cattle in *my* fields. Those farms sold out to me a while back.'

'So you're the cattle boss?'

Steve nodded. 'Doughty's my name. I'm boss since Pa died.'

Durant nodded. 'I thought you looked young.'

Steve's countenance altered. His eyes narrowed and his face set to a scowl. 'Are you saying I can't run the High S?'

'If you can or not isn't my business,' growled

Durant. 'My business is Luke Gray. Now, Mr Doughty, I'd sure like to know when my friend sold out and where he set to.'

Steve shrugged, though the discomfort in doing so showed in his face. 'That man you seek left, well. . . .' He glanced sharply at the black-haired one even then reining his mount round. 'It were maybe's three months back, weren't it, Tom?'

The other shook his head. 'I don't know about that.'

Steve's face clouded with confusion. 'But I thought—'

'I told you,' barked Tom. 'I don't know nothing.'

Steve stared intently at Durant. 'Green Ash was the last farm to sell up. As to where that man went I don't have a clue.'

Unease swamped Durant. 'You must've discussed stuff when you did the deal,' he protested. 'Hell, I mean, when you signed the deeds didn't he speak any on it?'

Steve looked furtively at Tom before muttering, 'I didn't speak to him at all.'

Durant stepped forward and grabbed the reins of Doughty's horse. 'Who in hell did? Damn it, who done a deal with Luke?'

Steve kicked out and struggled to get control of his horse. 'Get off,' he shouted. 'Get off my horse and get off my land.'

Durant released the leathers and tipped back his Stetson with a gloved hand.

'A name,' he snarled. 'Who agreed that sale with Luke?'

The man called Tom drew a pistol from his hip and clicked back the hammer. 'You heard it, feller, get off High S land lessen the full crew set to you. Heed that or you'll be sorry.'

Dragging their mounts about, the two men rode to the west.

Durant watched until they became specks in the distance. In no time, astride the mustang again, he suddenly felt the weariness borne of his advancing age. The journey he'd undertaken – two hundred miles across rough country – had taken its toll. It'd been a trek for sure and all, or so it seemed, for nothing.

He kicked his horse on. He ached for sheets and something more than the warm water of his canteen. He surveyed the flatland vastness ahead and made a decision. He'd take a break in Cooper's Town and try to decide what to do.

CHAPTER TWO

Cooper's Town lifted out of the parched landscape, its clapboard profile wide enough to suggest an established and decently populated settlement. What John Durant found was a community in decline – the settlement's main thoroughfare nothing more than a scarred and rutted earth street lined by boarded-up buildings. A few places still traded – a livery, a hardware store and a saloon called the Stage. All else bore padlocks on doors and wall paint peeling under the still-considerable heat of that late afternoon sun.

Slowing the horse to an amble, Durant noted the blank stares of folk on the boardwalks. In the past, through a roving career of law enforcement, he'd frequented places so isolated that in-comers met nothing short of the hostility those two High S men had meted out. This was different. These people had the countenances of mannequins; they were vacant, seemingly possessed of no emotion.

He dismissed his disquiet and halted the mustang. Soon, the horse sated from a trough and hitched, he made for the saloon. Inside, through a fug of smoke, he found a split-level and sparsely populated drinking establishment. Three men leant against the bar whilst two played cards at one of the tables.

Now, at the counter, he faced a portly barkeep of middle age.

Bert Lewis – past fifty and purveyor of drinks in Cooper's Town for two decades – studied his newest customer intently.

For his part, Durant took in the shotgun propped at the back of the bar and the pistol strapped to the barkeep's right hip.

'You tooled up for trouble?'

'It's best to be ready,' drawled Lewis. He tapped a finger to the revolver's butt. 'Even off I'm not a hotshot.'

Durant. shrugged. 'It's like that, is it?'

Lewis frowned. 'It's peaceable right now lessen you're set to start summat. It's different at night, mind.'

Durant sighed. 'I just want a beer.'

Lewis nodded and as he set to dispense the drink, Durant studied the two at the table – one a gangling young man of about twenty and the other older and wearing a battered white hat.

They both looked in his direction and Durant tipped a finger to the brim of his Stetson. 'And it's howdy to you, fellers.'

The younger man grinned inanely but the other scowled and sipped from a shot glass of dark-coloured liquor.

A slap on the counter made Durant turn and he grasped a flagon of beer and swallowed long. 'Hell, but I needed that.'

Lewis frowned. 'I'm Bert. You had a hot trail, eh?'

Durant nodded. 'The name's John Durant. It's hot as Hades and it takes a toll of a man. It don't help dodging slugs.'

Lewis sighed. 'Hell, someone tried to rob you?'

'No,' said Durant, 'a run-in with two cattlemen.'

A sharp scrape of a chair, audible even above the talk of the three men at the bar, had Durant glancing at the gangling youth and his gloomy-looking card partner. The former had risen to his feet and he now stood with indecision written across his face and his hands clutching the edge of the table.

Lewis shook his head. 'Where you bound, Vernon?'

The young man slid back into his seat.

'Goddamn lapdog,' spat the barkeep. Lewis poured a whiskey and slid it to Durant before saying confidentially and in a whispered tone, 'That half-wit is Vernon Glebe; the one with him is Frank Carling. They cut timber at Franklin's Forest.'

Durant shrugged, the relevance lost to him.

'Both are lackeys to our sheriff,' Lewis persisted. 'Makin will know you're in town soon enough. You'll get a visit.'

Durant laid the flagon aside and began to build a smoke. 'Good,' he intoned back. 'It'll save me looking the law up.'

'Say, what?' Lewis's countenance changed, his eyes

14

flashing bemusement. 'You'll be moved on.'

Durant drew deep on the smoke and shook his head. 'I'd reckon not. Well, leastways not till I find out where my friend is.'

Lewis shrugged. 'A Cooper's Town man was he?'

'No,' returned Durant, making no effort to modulate his own voice. 'He farmed out at a place called Green Ash.'

A loud gasp sounded from the card table and Durant turned to see Vernon Glebe scurrying toward the batwings. A second later, the swing doors clattering, the young man had gone.

Lewis frowned. 'Those men that jumped you – they were High S?'

Durant nodded. 'They rode at me with all guns blazing.'

Lewis looked around and then spat, 'They're a rough crew the High S. It didn't used to be so; young Steve's hired on some troublesome sorts. It's they that cause a ruckus at night.'

Durant jabbed a finger toward the batwings. 'This town seems kind of beat up. I suppose those hoodlums doing that?'

'Yeah,' growled Lewis. 'People leave this place fast; it's getting to be a risky stretch of life again.' The barkeep went quiet a moment, an intense look on his face. Finally, he muttered, 'All the small farmers are gone; they all sold out.'

Durant nodded. He downed the last dregs of beer from the flagon before placing it heavily on the bar. 'It sure sounds that way. Still, I'd seek to know the facts on Luke.'

'So you're setting to be in town a while?'

Durant nodded. 'Well – till I get some answers.'

Lewis stayed quiet and Durant cast a look around. He settled on that woodcutter Frank Carling who slumped in his seat with what seemed a dark expression. To one as experienced in such things as Durant was, Carling bore the look of a condemned man.

That very moment, the High S office rocked with shouts.

'Hell!' bellowed Harry Turner. 'Can't you see it, boy; can't you see how it's headed and has been for months?'

'I'm not a boy,' roared 22-year-old Steve Doughty. He shrugged away another man. 'Aw! Lay off, Cookie.'

Lyle Malone tied off the bandage at Steve's right arm and headed for a bowl to clean the blood off his hands.

'It's just a flesh nick,' the chuck man said with a grin.

'You're not getting a doc for me?' Steve wined.

'Doctor,' Cookie guffawed. 'In your pa's day—'

'My pa's day!' spat Steve. 'It's my day, goddamn it. I run the goddamn High S.'

Turner, a thickset man of fifty-one strode across and struck Steve across the face knocking him sideways off the sofa. The young ranch boss fell in a heap, sobbed and stayed there.

'You curb your mouth, boy,' barked Turner. 'I've

about had enough of it. You've changed some and none for the better.'

Steve stopped his crying and slowly got to his feet. 'I could fire you, Harry,' he warned tentatively.

'Do it,' bellowed Turner. 'Thirty years I sweated and bled for the High S. It wouldn't faze me a cent if you got rid of me.'

Steve slumped back on the sofa and ran his left hand to his aching face. 'You didn't have to belt me.'

Harry stared hard at Malone. 'Get back to the chuck house, Cookie. I've got to talk with Steve.'

With Malone gone, Harry pulled up a chair.

'You're the spit of your pa,' he said. 'But not like him.'

'But, Harry,' cried Steve. 'I've got to run it my way.'

'If running the High S into the ground is your way of doing it you're managing grand,' snapped Turner. 'I said not to take Riley Saunders on. He and those critters he rides with aren't right. Those beeves don't walk off on their own.'

'No proof,' barked Steve. 'You can't just accuse a feller.'

'I can,' growled Harry. 'I've been about enough to see how it is. He'll make a move on this place before long unless you get rid of him and his dogs. You've got to do it, Steve.'

'But, Harry,' protested the young man. 'He sealed the deals with them farmers didn't he?' He eyes widened then and he said reflectively, 'That feller what shot me was asking about that Green Ash sod-buster. Tom Leyton reckoned not to know of it.'

'That fits,' said Harry. 'Why'd you let Riley do it anyhow?'

'He said he'd got skills in that line,' snapped Steve.

'Good God, boy,' growled Harry. 'Your pa wouldn't give deals to his men; he'd do it face-to-face himself.'

'It's done now,' muttered Steve. 'High S is right bigger.'

'High S is right poorer for it,' retorted Harry. 'That bastard is laughing at you, Steve. He and his crew—'

'They're *my* crew,' retaliated Steve. 'They ride for me.'

'No, son,' drawled Harry. 'They ride for Riley. They're no good to the last of them and that's the end of it.'

Steve sat silent and brooding. Harry – unique in the High S ranks as he had a house in Cooper's Town – had known the young man since he'd been born; knew him well enough, of course, to recognize the pain in the young ranch boss's eyes.

'Listen, Steve,' said the veteran puncher. 'I spoke honest to your pa and I'll do the same now. You've had a go at holding the reins and messed up. You shouldn't have gone for those farms. They were trade to Cooper's Town and good neighbours. You've hired no-goods and it's got to be set right.'

Steve's eyes dampened. 'I just wish Pa was still here.'

'I know,' sighed Harry. 'But Liam's gone and what he built you got to keep. I mean, I take it Riley said to go shooting up on folk crossing our grass?'

Steve nodded. 'He says it's the only way we'll stamp down on drifters and saddle bums.'

'Hell,' spat Harry. 'There're more of them in our bunk house than cross our borders. My wife's a nervous wreck on account of Saunders and his lot shooting up the town at night.'

Steve looked desperate. 'Harry, I don't know what to do.'

'I'll clear out the scum. After that, we'll get new crew. We'll build up the brand again. We'll sell out them farms so we got smallholder's bringing life back to Cooper's Town.'

Steve gave a howl of frustration. 'They'll reckon me soft. I'm the High S boss and Riley says I'm the best there is.'

'You fool,' spat Harry. 'He'll fill your ears with that till the time comes to slit your throat. You've got to wise up, Steve, and see what's in front of your nose.'

Steve's face drained. 'So they don't reckon me much?'

'They reckon you a stupid pup,' growled Harry. 'They're calling you from one end of the range to the other. All the boys are saying it. Saul told me some of the stuff they brand you as.'

Steve looked crestfallen. 'I just don't—'

'I wouldn't lie, Steve,' cut in Harry. 'I'm as good as kin to you. I'll tell you straight. Riley Saunders is planning summat bad and that dog wouldn't give spit for you.'

'I'll fire them all,' raged Steve. 'I'll tell *that* to them!'

Harry groaned. 'Stay your horses, boy. Do that and we'll bury you tomorrow! No, we need to do it right. I've got to get our people set, so we keep our peace till time's right.'

Steve looked forlorn. 'What're you saying, Harry?'

'For now,' growled Harry. 'Riley thinks he's got the top hand; but, by God, the clock is ticking on that bastard!'

In the Stage Saloon, Bert Lewis frowned, still not recalling the man this silver-haired stranger sought.

'I can't recollect this Luke Gray,' he said. 'That's not saying he didn't drink in here.' He glanced to the three men further along the bar. 'Hey, Saw Bone, you got a moment?'

An oldster approached. 'What is it, Bert?'

'A man what farmed Green Ash; you mind who I'm saying on?'

The old boy was silent a moment before he said croakily, 'Aye, right enough I recall that man. Real quiet he were when you'd see him in town. He was about last to make a deal with Doughty a few months back.'

Durant considered the dilapidated state of Green Ash farm and supposed a place, untended, could fall to that state of disrepair in such a period.

'I got told Luke sold out?' said Durant. 'That right?'

'Sure is,' drawled the old timer. 'I heard he set further west. I heard say he mentioned on 'Frisco.'

'San Francisco!' exclaimed Durant. 'God alive,

that's not Luke Gray. He thought Morton was too much in the busy way; there isn't a chance in hell he'd set to a city that size. Anyway, he wrote me he'd be farming that place till he died.'

The old man shrugged. 'I'm just saying what I heard. That man you're after – like I said, he spoke mostly to no one. It's what I heard and that's that!'

Durant felt rage surge. 'Damn it, who'd you hear it off?'

The oldster turned away and Durant grabbed at the back of the ancient's shirt. 'Answer me!'

Frank Carling moved fast. He prodded Durant's face with the muzzle of a Colt and growled, 'Let Saw Bone be, mister.'

Durant released his grip and nodded. 'Bed your weapon, feller, there's no harm done.'

Frank Carling slid his pistol back into its holster. 'You're pushing for trouble, mister. You beat up on old timers.'

'I just held him by the shirt,' retorted Durant.

'He's old,' barked Carling. 'He don't need that.'

Durant nodded. 'I apologize on that. It's just I'm shook up some with my friend being gone.'

Carling scowled. 'And you'll be gone and all. You ain't welcome; saddle up and ride out.'

'D'you mind if I finish my beer?' said Durant. He was playing it soft. When Carling hadn't answered Durant added, 'Ah, c'mon feller? I'm just parched like a dried creek and haven't seen hard drink for that long. I'll be no more bother.'

'God's teeth,' Carling sneered. 'Goddamn, yeller

saddle bum. Right, finish your drink, but I'll be watching. You hear?'

Durant nodded and he sidled back to the counter.

Bert Lewis pinned Durant with a look of bemusement. 'I got to say, I weren't expecting hassle from you!'

Durant frowned. 'Sorry about that. I'll behave now.'

Lewis sighed. 'I'd reckon, feller, that unless you get scarce Makin will definitely be paying you a visit.'

Durant took a sup of the beer. 'Really,' he said as he lowered the glass. He drew a sleeve over his froth-bound lips. 'Is that a goddamn fact?'

CHAPTER THREE

Blair Makin maintained his vigil behind the jailhouse desk whilst, at the window, Vernon Glebe scanned for the stranger's exit from the saloon.

'Hell, Sheriff,' said Vernon loudly when Durant hadn't showed. 'He's a big enough mister, right enough.'

Makin nodded but stayed silent. He'd seen this Durant arrive, a gut-churning experience for the Cooper's Town sheriff. Some men have presence – an air of menace even as they ride – and this Durant possessed it in buckets. He sat tall in the saddle, his muscular six-foot frame attired in dusty range gear. Under a tipped back Stetson, Durant's silver hair flowed in impressive locks whilst his equally tinted moustache seemed to score a face bronzed and creased with sun and middle age. Durant looked impressive, Sheriff Makin admitted to himself.

The sheriff shoved his papers aside. Vernon's information about the stranger's search for a farmer friend was worrying.

Makin began to muse on recent happenings but Vernon's anxious voice dragged him back.

'Hell, Sheriff. You'll be running that feller out?'

Makin lifted a Colt Peacemaker out of the desk drawer and jabbed in Vernon's direction. 'Tell me again,' said Makin, 'what that feller said.'

'Ah, hell,' whined Vernon. 'Can't I get back to my drink?'

Makin clicked back the Colt's hammer and levelled the gun. 'Goddamn you, Vernon; tell me or else!'

Vernon paled. 'I said already – he's seeking that Green Ash feller. He spoke summat about cattlemen shooting.'

Makin eased the hammer back and he shook his head. 'Who the hell is this silver-hair?'

Vernon gulped and inched toward the door. He planned to bolt out but the arrival of another made him freeze.

Mayor Thomas Lassiter stalked into the jailhouse. At fifty-three Lassiter had been the settlement's lead official for over a decade, most of which time he'd felt pride and a sense of achievement in the task. These last few months, though, all that had altered.

When Sheriff Makin greeted his arrival with a grunt, Lassiter pulled out a seat and dropped on to it.

'I'm busy,' snarled Makin, his eyes full of contempt.

'Yeah,' Lassiter snapped, 'busy doing nothing as usual.'

'What's your problem?'

'You'll holster that mouth,' barked Lassiter.

'Lessen you've forgot it's us town folk what pay your wages.'

Makin glared but held his tongue. Lassiter glanced around and noticed Vernon. 'Get out, you fool!'

Vernon nodded and shot into the street.

'What's he want?' spat Lassiter.

Makin shrugged. 'He's got his uses.'

'He's no more use than you are right now. I've just heard more families are set to leave. I want changes, damn it, Makin!'

'Changes?' challenged the sheriff. 'What the hell—'

'A curb on thugs,' cut in Lassiter. 'Good people are scared when they're about. I'm looking to a deputy soon as I can.'

'I'm sheriff,' snapped Makin. 'I don't need no assistant.'

'So help me I'll do it,' barked Lassiter. 'If you won't or can't get this town in order I'll damn well get me a deputy.'

Makin's features set grim. 'I'll do it, don't worry.'

'One thing more,' Lassiter said. 'You'll start stocking them cells when laws are broke.'

'I know best,' retorted Makin. 'A sheriff needs to—'

'He needs to tread steady,' drawled Lassiter standing up. 'I best see some smiling locals, Sheriff, or they'll be changes. You hear me on that?'

Lassiter stalked out and Makin cursed the town official to hell. Changes, he mulled furiously, there would be those right enough.

*

Dusk was descending as Durant finally left the saloon. Lightheaded but not quite drunk, he led his horse to the livery. The oldster who ran the place – a wrinkle-faced aged called Abel Field – took Durant's money and nodded without comment.

Now, mid-way down Liberty Row, Durant studied the Bellfield Hotel. His heart sank. This building – set over four floors and with a balustrade balcony running the entire length of the upper exterior – was padlocked shut and wore a sign reading: For Sale.

Durant groaned. He'd ask the liveryman if he could sleep in the hayloft. He half-turned when a voice pulled him up.

'It's been closed for months now.'

A woman stood there, a shawl about her shoulders and a fretful look on her face. Her hair was dark, her eyes, slate grey, regarded him intently. She was middle-aged, Durant assessed, and a handsome woman at that.

'Pa and me gave it up,' she went on. 'We couldn't make it work when things started to change.'

He nodded. 'Thank you, ma'am, I'll make other arrangements.'

She stepped close and her frown became disapproving. 'Liquored-up at this hour,' she rebuked. 'It's disgusting!

Durant shook his head. 'I've had a bad day,' he said. 'I've ridden hundreds of miles and I—'

She turned and called out, 'Pa!'

Across the way, a door creaked open and an elderly face appeared. 'What is it, Annie?'

'This man here ain't got nowhere to stay.'

The old man appraised Durant and nodded. 'You can use our shack for a small sum, feller. It's at the end of this street.'

The woman proffered Durant a key. 'You can't miss it.'

He nodded. 'I'd be obliged if you'd point me the way of an eat house; I haven't had more than saddle fare for days.'

She shook her head. 'It's all gone from Cooper's Town.' She looked him up and down. 'I'm sorry.'

He shrugged and began to walk off.

'Wait a moment,' she shouted after him. 'It'd be a while, then . . . since a good meal?'

He nodded. 'It's been a time; it's been a long ride.'

'Be back at eight,' she said. 'That's when I serve dinner. It'll just be stew but it'll soak out some of the liquor.'

Durant grinned and walked on. At last on this regrettable day of shock news and unreceptive company, he'd found a person he liked.

They rode into Cooper's Town as the saloon's tallboy clock clicked its hands to 8 p.m. Now, sprawled on the raised section's wing-back chairs, Clem Daly swigged from a whiskey bottle before passing it to Tom Leyton. All the gang were there that night, some building smokes and others checking their guns.

The rest of the ranch-hands – long-serving punchers and ropers loyal to the Doughty brand – were back at the High S, finishing their evening meal or out night hawking. They could talk safely.

Riley Saunders – 180lbs of wanted Nebraska criminal – shook his head. 'Hell's teeth, Tom. You let that saddle bum get away.'

Tom lowered the whiskey from his lips and scowled. 'He had the cover, Riley. That feller could shoot some too. Scarred that darn fool kid Steve right enough.'

'That saddle bum should've dead-eyed Doughty,' drawled Clem. 'It'd save us the job.'

Riley shook his head. 'Not till he's signed over them deeds. We need to keep that scurvy pup alive till then.'

Riley spat at the floorboards and considered their tenure at the High S. They'd crossed to these lands months before and happened upon Cooper's Town. A chance meeting with Doughty had brought rich rewards. The young cattle boss had been desperate for hands – most of the High S crew leaving after the death of the former patriarch Liam Doughty. Steve took Riley's mob on as seen.

Manna from heaven granted to the outlaws. They'd pulled this ruse before; up north, they'd spent months working a brand before slaughtering the ranch boss and his family after they'd signed over the deeds. Afterwards, they'd driven the cattle out to any buyer at any price and with punchers like Leyton in the ranks, altering the marks came with the deal.

Riley was eager to conclude business now. He'd curried favour with Steve Doughty – even sealing the line of small farms bordering the High S eastern border that the novice cattle boss craved. Most of the sodbusters had agreed quickly, threats sufficing. That last one at Green Ash had been a problem, though. He hadn't been cowed; he'd resisted defiantly all the way.

A call from Clem pulled Riley out of his musings.

'Cookie spoke of a ruckus between Steve and Turner. Seems they went at it some but Malone couldn't rightly say what.'

'That Turner's on to us,' growled Riley. 'I reckon he'll need to have a little accident.'

Men exchanged furtive glances.

'Like that sodbuster at Green Ash?' Clem drawled. He cast aside the whiskey bottle he'd snatched back and duly emptied. It clattered to the floor and only when it silenced did Clem add, 'Hey, Tom – you say that drifter what nicked Doughty were asking about one of them farmers?'

'Yeah,' said Leyton sombrely. 'That man at Green Ash.'

Clem sighed and muttered quietly, 'Christ, but he screamed.'

'So would you with your ears cut off,' said Leyton. He screwed his face up, always appalled when someone mentioned the torture. 'Where in hell did you learn that little trick, Riley?'

'I heard a feller name of Vicious Bill in Missouri done it,' Riley smirked. 'I weren't sure I had it in me. Still, once you get going it's not so bad.'

'Not for you,' spluttered Leyton. 'That man suffered some.'

Riley dragged a knife out of his belt and gestured it toward Leyton. 'You want some, boy?'

A raucous burst of laughter followed.

'Goddamn it,' barked Leyton. 'I'm with the crew, aren't I?'

Riley slid the knife back and smirked. 'We're gonna have to move soon. This place makes me sick.'

'This drifter asking on Green Ash,' queried Clem. 'You reckon there's a worry there?'

Riley shook his head. 'The saddle bum will be long gone. No problem I'd say. Mind, I reckon we still got to get a pace on.'

'What you thinking?' questioned Clem.

'It'll be the same as last time,' returned Riley. 'We'll force Doughty to sign over the deeds, get rid of him then sell off the cattle. We'll head south then.'

'That kid boss will sign at the first ask,' scoffed Clem. 'Won't be any need for your knife.'

Riley shook his head and his eyes took on that glazed look they all feared.

'Maybe not to get that stupid pup to sign,' he said with menace to his words. 'But I got to say I just like to have them bleed and scream.'

CHAPTER FOUR

After a fine meal and, surprisingly, sipping a brandy Anne had provided, Durant said, 'That was a grand eat, ma'am. My wife Emma could do a stew just as—'

'Emma?' she cut in.

'My late wife,' he said sombrely. 'Fever took her.'

'Oh, I'm so sorry,' she uttered, shaking her head. 'I know how it feels. My own husband's dead near six years now.'

'Goddamn drunk, he was,' growled Old Ned.

Durant nodded. Anne's comments earlier made sense now.

'Your wife,' said Anne. 'That brought you here?'

He explained everything then. At the age of forty-six, with two decades behind the badge, with a grown-up daughter and a dead wife, he'd been through it all. Every joy and agony had spanned his lifetime. He'd been a devoted marshal, committed to the service's ideals; ready to tackle any challenge.

31

Luke Gray was different. He was darn good at the job but his heart just wasn't in it. He'd resigned and headed west. They'd promised to keep in touch – Luke vowing to write to give details of the farm he'd bought, Durant pledging to respond quickly and visit. Then the letter arrived to say Luke had found his Nirvana.

Circumstances intervened, though. The death of Emma had brought Durant's entire world crashing down around his ears. Months passed by before he'd even started the process of grief. He'd returned to work a driven and increasingly reckless man. Some hinted he'd developed a death wish. Finally, the powers-that-be acted. He'd been retired and thanked by the grateful citizenry of Morton for his long and tireless service. Disgruntled, he'd set out to find Luke Gray.

'Seems this Gray got an offer he couldn't say no to,' Old Ned said as Durant finished. 'All them sodbusters sold out, I heard. If the money didn't tempt them then Doughty's men—'

Ned stopped short as a gun blast sounded in onc of the nearby streets and instinct drove Durant to his feet, his right hand clutching the butt of his Colt.

'It's OK,' reassured Anne. 'It's High S men getting rowdy about the saloon. It'll quiet just past midnight. Trouble was the stage passengers didn't like it and kept complaining and before long, the stage company struck Cooper's Town off the route. That's why the hotel and the other businesses closed.'

'Your sheriff,' said Durant, his annoyance clear. 'Why don't he put a stop to it?'

Old Ned scowled. 'He's a useless piece of—'

'Pa!' bellowed Anne. She fixed Durant with an intrigued stare. 'Pa's got a coarse tongue but he's right enough. Sheriff Makin's neither use nor ornament to Cooper's Town. He lets them High S do what they like. I reckon he's just plain scared but I can't blame the man for that.'

'They ride in, drink a heap then blast slugs in Main Street,' growled Old Ned. 'There've been a few killings too.'

Durant shook his head. 'Anyone get tried for that?'

'Hell no,' scoffed Old Ned. 'It gets wrote off. There's a few in town talk tough but they're all scared of the High S.'

'Hush, Pa,' said Anne. 'It don't do to call those cattle men.' She looked anxiously at Durant. 'We just don't know—'

'Ma'am,' he said. 'I shot a High S feller on the way in. If it's a list of people they ain't happy with I'll be top of it.'

'Dang,' cried Ned. 'Which one you kill? Were it Riley?'

Durant shook his head. 'I winged a feller called Doughty.'

'Steve?' exclaimed Anne. 'He owns the High S now.'

Durant frowned. 'So he said. He told me his fellers settled the sale deal on Green Ash.'

'If that was Riley,' replied Old Ned. 'It would be settled right enough. He's a nasty piece of work. My advice, Durant, is forget your friend. He'll have rooted elsewhere. Head home, that'd be best.'

Durant sighed and put his glass aside. 'What's best now is sleep.' He stifled a yawn and climbed wearily to his feet. 'You've been so kind.'

Anne smiled back sweetly before they exited to the boardwalk where their eyes locked. An instant later, as that gaze held, he felt a surge of longing. He gulped it out and thought guiltily of his dead wife. He doffed his hat and walked down the steps on to the street.

He walked on then but glanced back. Anne held her pose on the boardwalk. She let him turn completely before offering a wave and plunging back into her house.

Durant breathed deeply. Then headed for bed.

Riley glanced at the clock: 11 p.m. A few of his men kept guard on the boardwalk outside the saloon; they'd been loosing slugs on and off for hours to relieve the boredom.

The Stage had gradually filled – mostly locals but a couple of faces Riley didn't recognize. Two men had entered together, a couple of bearded, sturdy fellers wearing coats and dust-dressed hats. They were probably drifters passing through but you just never could tell.

Riley had studied them for a while, noting the increasing volume of whiskey both consumed. Now, as one swaggered about the saloon, Riley's anger began to rise.

'Hell,' spat the drunken stranger, shoving several of the clientele aside. 'There's got to be some goddamn feller willing to risk a few dollars with me and Jake.'

Bert Lewis had a hand to his revolver but he eased it away as Riley stepped deliberately down the raised area's steps.

'I'll play some poker with you, mister.'

The liquored-up stranger grinned and nodded at his partner. 'Hear that, Jake? This skinny feller's got greenbacks to burn.'

The other nodded. 'I hear you, Riker.'

The one called Riker dragged off his hat and slapped it against an empty table. 'We'll set right here and get to it.'

Riley shook his head and pointed to the rear of the saloon. 'We got us a special card room out back, fellers.'

Riker shrugged. 'So long's the redeye's flowing.'

A moment later, Riker and Jake staggered after Riley toward a door in the saloon's rear wall.

Bert Lewis shook his head and grabbed for a bottle of whiskey and some shot tumblers. In the card room, he deposited the bottle and glasses on the baize-topped table and lit a kerosene lamp. Then he retreated to the door as Riley and the two men sat down.

'You can go,' drawled Riley without looking at the barkeep.

Lewis departed then, shutting the door behind him.

'Now, fellers,' smirked Riley. 'It'll be a five card game.' He tapped out the cards from the packet. 'I goddamn love this stud to death!'

In Cooper's Town jailhouse the glowing light of a kerosene lamp illuminated their worried faces.

'But boys,' drawled Makin. 'I got the mayor busting my hide on one hand; this silver-haired feller's asking questions on the other. I mean, what'll I say? I can only put it as it happened. Hell, you come back here saying you've found a body!'

'I ain't worried none on that silver-hair,' spat Frank Carling. 'He pissed himself when I shoved my gun in his face. As for you, Sheriff – jeez, you'd drop me and Vern in it?'

Vernon's face was set grim. He shuddered, recalling a misty morning months ago as he and Frank delivered timber. Frank had reined the wagon horses up and pointed to something in the distance. They both watched in silence as mounted men left Green Ash Farm at the gallop. Vernon had recognized them all.

When those riders had cleared, Frank moved the wagon on and they'd made that shocking discovery. Inside, Luke Gray, tied to a chair, bore the scars and injuries of a horrific death.

Vernon swallowed and fought down the bile that touched at the back of his throat. He clamped his eyes shut now, trying to blank the image that still haunted at nights.

The sheriff – when eventually alerted – had shown little surprise. He made Vernon and Frank go back. They'd do as told: losing the cadaver; storing the planks in the yard before disposing of the body in the pine forest where they worked. Then, strangely, Makin had paid for the timber.

Vernon opened his eyes and locked Makin with a look of horror. 'You know who done that killing. We said what we saw.'

Makin shook his head and shrugged. 'I only got your word on that. Whether a hanging judge would take it as Gospel, well, you just can't say.'

'You bastard,' Carling barked. 'You stinking piece of scum!'

'Now,' retorted Makin with a grin. 'I always said I'll protect you best I can.'

Makin frowned. He knew the truth of it right enough. He – sheriff of that jurisdiction – had been out at Gray's farm the evening before the two wood mill assistants had discovered the body. Gray had reported increasing intimidation from the High S men and Makin set out to discuss the matter.

Whilst there, High S men turned up. Riley, in drink, was volatile. At one point, the psychopath turned on Makin.

Makin had survived by pleading on his knees. He felt no shame at abandoning Gray to his awful fate; no shame at how he'd debased himself and begged to live. Survival came first.

Finally, given permission to leave by Riley but with

a foreboding warning of merciless retribution if he ever spoke or got in the High S man's way and to return and dispose of the body the next day, Makin fled back to Cooper's Town. But not before Riley had secured the sheriff's silence. He'd thrust a knife at the lawman and ordered him to inflict the first cut. Makin had done it – blanking Gray's pitiful screams – before riding hell for leather away from there.

The sheriff had cursed that fateful morning. The fact of Glebe and Carling finding the body had been bad enough. The realization that Riley and his thug friends had stayed in Green Ash all night torturing that poor bastard until he signed the deeds had been a greater shock.

From that day to this he'd let High S men do what they wanted; he moved drifters on for fear they'd dig around and discover even the smallest clue.

Carling's banging of a fist on the jailhouse desk roused Makin from his inner mulling.

'We've done your bidding long enough,' barked the older wood mill man. 'If federals; US army or the goddamn Pinkertons turn up – you've got to stand by me and Vernon, Sheriff.'

'I'll do what I can,' retorted Makin. 'We've just got to hope this silver-haired stranger moves on quick. We got to hope he don't hang around asking more questions and boys' – he fixed Frank and Vernon with a scorching glare – 'we best hope those High S boys don't get to hear you're putting them in the frame for murder.'

38

Vernon and Carling trudged out of the jailhouse in silence. Makin took a deep breath and reached for the whiskey bottle.

CHAPTER FIVE

Riley lay his cards aside, perusing the rewardingly high pile of dollar bills on the table by his right hand. This had been easy pickings – two men with enough whiskey in them were reckless with their bets and slow of thought.

Riker shook his head. 'What the hell're you doing?'

Riley yawned. 'I'm set for my bed.'

Riker's nostrils flared and a muscle in his jaw twitched noticeably. 'I don't reckon so, feller.'

Riley scooped up the money and stuffed it into the pocket of his pants. 'Say, what?'

Riker slammed a fist down on to the table, making the bottle and glasses jump. 'Get that money back on this table, boy!'

Riley rose to his feet slowly, adjusting the brim of his hat with one hand and letting the other rest loosely on the gun at his right hip.

'Take your stinking carcases back to the gutter where you belong,' he said icily. 'Thanks for the money, mind.'

Riker shot up and lunged for his gun. It didn't clear the holster.

Riley drew with a practised speed, Colt .44 to hand and flame ripping out of the muzzle. The slug bit into Riker's chest and drove him fast into the wall. He held upright a moment, hands clutching uselessly at the bloody hole before he slid to the floor where he lay open-eyed but motionless.

Jake, his hands raised now, shook his head. With a forced smile he gasped, 'Right you are, feller. You'll get no trouble from me.'

Riley nodded and strode to the door. He gripped the handle but then looked back.

'Hell's teeth,' he spat. 'I almost forgot summat!'

'What?' Jake uttered pensively.

Riley sighed and levelled the Colt. 'No witnesses,' he said softly before blasting a bullet between Jake's eyes. The chair and the lifeless form of Jake slammed backward on to the floor and Riley slid the gun to its holster. He grinned. 'Nice doing business with you, boys!'

Durant prepared to undress – the gun blasts having faded from the town shortly past 1 a.m. – when a rapping at the shack's door took him by surprise. He found Anne out there in the dark street, a pile of towels in her arms.

'I forgot to give you these,' she said shakily. 'There's a tin tub out back and if you get a fire up in the morning you can boil a bath up.'

41

He glanced quickly to a cabinet against the wall and saw a heap of towelling neatly folded. Is it, he mused, that she just wanted an excuse to visit him?

'Your pa?'

'He's fast asleep, I'll just—'

'Please, Anne,' he said, opening the door fully. 'Call me John.'

She stepped in and held her gaze down. 'I'll put these on the side and—'

'No, ma'am,' he hissed through gritted teeth. 'I thank you for the shack; I'm mighty obliged for that fine meal you cooked. But, Goddamn it, my Emma weighs heavy on me.'

She stumbled back toward the door, her look one of abject embarrassment. 'Oh, dear Lord, I'm so sorry.'

'Stop,' he bellowed. 'Mrs Slocum, would you kindly stop.'

She halted in the doorway and looked like she would cry.

He strode across and gently eased her in.

'I'm sorry,' he said softly.

'What for?' she exclaimed, 'for thinking of your late wife?'

'Anne,' he said breathlessly. 'I haven't looked nor thought of another woman since my Emma passed.' He breathed in deeply. 'Until now, that is.'

She trembled. 'What're you saying, Mr Durant?'

He lifted the towels off her and threw them on to the bed. A second later, they met like magnets in a passionate, lingering kiss. When it ended, her whole body trembling she gasped, 'It's just—'

He placed a forefinger to her lips. 'I thought I might never get past Emma,' he said quietly. 'I guess it just happens.'

'Stay a while, John,' she pleaded. 'I really want you to.'

'I've got to stay, Anne.' His eyes narrowed. 'This thing with Luke isn't right. Old Saw Bone said Luke had sold up and set out to San Francisco. There's no way that happened.'

She nodded. 'Where is he then?'

'For now,' he sighed, 'I just want to think of you. Tomorrow – I'll go looking for Luke.'

The saloon had cleared by the time Makin got in there. He'd waited until the High S men mounted up and left town before reaching for a gun and crossing the street.

Bert Lewis, his face pale, was slouched over the bar. He regarded Makin with a look of distain. 'I'd not reckon you'd hurry to a murder, Sheriff?' He shook his head. 'The card room!'

Makin stepped across and peered in. He surveyed the blood-spattered floor and walls and the cadavers of two strangers. He stepped in, fighting bile that rose in his throat and he rummaged through each man's pockets. He extracted money and papers that might identify them and shoved the lifted items in his own coat.

Back in the bar, he gestured for a drink.

Bert Lewis delivered a glass of redeye and Makin

lingered on it.

'There ain't a thing on them fellers to say who they were, Bert,' drawled the sheriff. 'Just a couple of nameless drifters.' He eyed the barkeep with a caustic glare. 'You said murder; you see it happen then?'

'Hell, no,' spat the barkeep. 'It happened behind a closed door.' Bert shrugged. 'There was only Riley Saunders and them poor bastards in there.'

Makin eyes flashed. 'What did Riley say?'

'Does it matter any?'

Makin sighed. 'Probably not; still – you'd best say.'

Bert put a towel over one of the beer pumps and fixed the sheriff with a disbelieving stare. 'He reckoned' – the barkeep said laconically – 'them fellers was that cut up at losing they both shot themselves.'

Makin gulped down the whiskey and made for the batwings.

'That's it?' sputtered Lewis. 'You're just walking out.'

'Lock that room for the night,' growled Makin stepping on to the boardwalk. 'I'll get Albert to collect the bodies in the morning. He can have their guns; I'll get their horses sorted somehow.' He looked back and shook his head. 'The mayor will raise sweet hell when he hears of it.'

Later, back in the jailhouse, he penned the report. At the foot of the page, he scribbled . . . suicide.

CHAPTER SIX

Alone, when Anne left in the still, quiet hours, Durant slept soundly. Late morning had arrived by the time he'd woken, lit a fire and boiled water from a well in the street to fill the tub. There were supplies enough in a cupboard to make up breakfast and after a smoke, he lay there in the soapy enfold of steaming water, all the aches and trail dust dispelled. By midday, he'd dressed again and headed out.

Ten minutes later, a spur of the moment decision, he strode in through the open door of the jailhouse.

Sheriff Makin glanced up from papers on his desk as Durant's solid footfalls sounded on the plank floor.

Without waiting for an invite, Durant lifted off his Stetson and dropped into a chair. He fixed the Cooper's Town lawman with a firm stare. 'I'm John Durant.'

The sheriff nodded. 'And I'm Makin. I heard you touched town yesterday.'

Durant shrugged. 'I heard you'd be paying me a visit.'

Makin leant back in his seat and sighed. 'How long you staying, Durant?'

'Until I get answers I'm happy with!'

'Word is you've been asking about Green Ash,' growled the sheriff. 'Fact is, mister, that farm like all the others sold out to High S. Doughty's got the deeds to prove it.'

'Well,' said Durant gruffly. 'Things I've heard about Luke Gray don't seem to add up. I don't intend to leave untill I'm satisfied why and where he went. I'll speak with these High S boys in due course.'

'High S,' gasped Makin. 'Why'd you want to talk to them?'

'One of them must've sealed the sale with Luke. That Steve Doughty seemed right confused over that point, I got to say.'

Makin paled. 'You've spoke to Doughty?'

Durant explained about the incident the day before.

Makin shook his head then. 'That's clear, then. They won't talk with you, Durant. I'd reckon you should saddle up and go back to where you hailed from. You been told that Gray feller sold up and rode off. Let your head settle on that some.'

'Talking of settling,' drawled Durant then, 'I didn't sleep too good last night on account of folk loosing slugs. You don't put a stop to that?'

'It ain't a problem,' barked the sheriff.

Another voice broke in loudly. 'Like hell it's not!'

Durant turned to see a man bustle in off the street. The thinning-haired personage wearing a pair of slacks and a checked shirt nodded. 'I'm Thomas Lassiter, mayor of this dung hole. I've just been told you used to be a federal?'

Durant's heart sank. God's teeth – that meant either Anne or her father had revealed their discussion the previous evening. He felt anger surge but it soon subsided when he mused on Anne. He couldn't blame her. He'd developed intense feelings for her and if she felt the same way, which he sensed she did, she'd probably said it in excitement rather than a lack of confidentially. Durant studied Makin, noting the sheriff's sagged posture and a face etched with despair.

Fixing his gaze on Lassiter, Durant said, 'Yeah, I marshalled once back in Missouri.'

'Well, mister,' announced the mayor with a pleading look in his eyes. 'There're a few folks in town would like to hire you.'

Durant shook his head. 'Hire me?'

'Absolutely,' returned Lassiter, 'to be our deputy.'

'Now just hang on there!' Makin barked out.

Lassiter jabbed a finger at the sheriff. 'I told you what would happen unless you curbed those High S thugs. My chickens are laying square eggs on account of shooting and now I hear of killing in the Stage.' Lassiter wiped his sweat-beaded brow with the back of one hand. He blew out his cheeks, strain and worry evident in his face. 'This ex-federal wants the job,' he added with a nod at Durant. 'Then by God he'll have it.'

Durant pondered the offer. He fixed Makin with

47

an inquisitive glare. 'There was a murder in the saloon?'

'Double murder!' barked Lassiter. 'Two drifters shot in the card room.'

'Now, steady there,' growled Makin waving the report he'd completed. 'I got witnesses enough to say one of them fellers was drunk and right unstable. Seems the two of them played poker and got into an argument. One killed the other then shot himself in remorse.'

'My aunt's eyes!' spat Lassiter. 'They'll be High S written all over this but getting people to say so isn't going to happen.'

Durant became resolved. A law badge might help get the answers he sought. He climbed to his feet and offered a hand to the mayor. 'I'll accept, Mayor; I'll start right now.'

Lassiter shook warmly. 'Dang,' the town official said. 'Wait till people hear. They'll be right pleased.'

The mayor hurried away and Durant replaced his hat. He held out an open palm and, scowling, Makin reached into his desk drawer. He pulled out a tin badge and slapped it into Durant's hand.

'You could regret this,' the sheriff drawled. 'Pin that on and it'll all change.'

Durant fixed the badge to his vest and tapped a finger to the butt of his Colt. 'I'd reckon as much.'

Anne's wide eyes reflected her shock and horror.

'John, what have you done?' she gasped.

'Makin's not gonna like that,' muttered Ned.

48

'Having a proper lawman about Cooper's Town will make trouble for him.'

Durant nodded. 'It seems that's the mayor's way of thinking; he hired me on. In fact, everyone I've spoken to since I've been in Cooper's Town has said the same. This place is wasting away and that sheriff is letting it happen.'

Old Ned nodded. 'I reckon you're done right, son.'

'Pa,' snapped Anne. 'Get coffee. I'll speak to John.'

The oldster shuffled away into the kitchen and Anne clutched at Durant. 'Why d'you do it? Why put yourself in harm's way?'

He grinned. 'Anne, a law badge it's all I've known.'

'But you're retired,' she protested. 'There is no need to—'

'I'll be OK,' he cut in softly. 'Besides, a badge might get me to the truth about Luke.'

She nodded then, her countenance grim. 'You're convinced your friend didn't just sell up and leave, aren't you?'

'From what Luke wrote,' said Durant sourly, 'I'd reckon it's the last thing he'd do unless someone persuaded him otherwise.'

Anne pulled away and sank into a seat. 'Surely too much time's passed,' she said. 'Your friend sold out months back and I just can't see how you'll find anything out.'

Durant shrugged. 'I've got to try. I owe Luke that.'

Old Ned returned with the coffee and Durant

49

sipped at his mug reflectively. He would ask about town if folk had met and talked to Luke. He would start with all the trade people. He pondered on that pile of decent timber stacked neatly at the side of Green Ash farm.

'Anne,' he said then, 'Bert told me of a wood mill.'

She nodded. 'That's Garside's out at Franklin's Forest. It's a few miles north of town.' She looked confused. 'Why—'

'Oh, it's nothing probably,' he cut in. He rose, slid on his hat and turned to leave.

'Your dinner?' said Anne. 'You'll be here at eight again?'

He smiled in reply. 'Wild horses couldn't stop me!'

Makin sat at his desk, his face a picture of disgruntlement as Durant entered the jailhouse that hot afternoon.

The new deputy went straight to the long cabinet and withdrew a Spencer carbine. He lifted a cartridge from the shelf and slid it into the chamber of the rifle.

'Get your hide at home, why don't you?' scowled Makin. 'Go where you need; take what you want.' His eyes flashed his anger.

Durant shook his head. 'I intend to, Makin. I intend to get in the faces of a few hereabouts.'

'Watch your step, Durant,' the sheriff spat through gritted teeth. 'I got made to take you on but I don't like it.'

'You'll find me reliable in a ruckus,' answered Durant. 'And I'll deal with trouble if I see it.'

Makin's eyes pinned Durant with a stare of warning. 'There's some best left alone in this town.'

Durant shrugged. 'High S men you mean?'

'You push too much you won't like what comes back.'

'I ain't afraid to try.'

Makin shook his head. 'It's your funeral, mister.'

'I reckon not,' Durant drawled. He threw a disparaging look at the sheriff and then stepped towards the door.

'Where in hell you going?' barked Makin.

'I said I'd get at my friend's leaving of Green Ash and I'll start right now.'

'Say what?' gasped Makin. 'What you gonna do?'

Durant shrugged. 'I met two fellers in the saloon yesterday – names of Glebe and Carling. I didn't reckon it at the time but I heard they work at some wood mill. Luke Gray had fresh timber stacked at his farm and I reckoned to ask those men about that.'

Makin sat stony-faced a moment before muttering, 'Now, stay a bit, Durant. Those boys are working hard at the mill, Garside won't take well you bothering them. They'll be back come nightfall.'

Durant shrugged. Makin's presentation had changed now. He stayed seated but a fidgety restlessness had overtaken him. The pallor of the sheriff's face had definitely altered, his skin had paled and his eyes constantly shifted. Makin hauled a whiskey bottle out of the desk drawer.

'Here,' he said. 'We got off wrong. A shot with me, eh?'

Durant retraced his steps and sank back on to the seat. A moment later, he sipped the fiery fluid and observed the sheriff over the rim of a shot glass.

'We got to stop this slug-loosing at night.'

Makin shrugged. 'I guessed as much.' He shook his head. 'We're both likely to get blasted while we're doing it.'

'We're the law,' Durant said. 'It's what we get paid for.'

'I don't know where you were a federal,' spat the sheriff testily. 'But out here near the border, law's a goddamn different thing. You're law because people let you be. You need an easy way; you deal with stuff by word and trust.'

'I'm easy,' returned Durant. 'But quick if I'm riled.'

Makin shrugged. 'There's a plot open in the grave-yard.' The sheriff took a liberal swallow of the redeye and looked quizzically as he drawled, 'I meant to ask – where you staying? I mean, the hotel's shut.'

'I'm renting a shack.'

Makin shook his head. 'A shack, you say? Only place I know of is Old Ned Slocum's place on Liberty.'

When Durant remained tight-lipped, the sheriff grinned. 'Fine gal he's got there. Yes sir, I'd sure like to get through a cold night warming some sheets with her.'

Rage drove Durant forward. He'd belted the glass out of Makin's hand before the sheriff knew what hit him and a moment later, Durant's hand gripping his throat, Makin found himself slammed back against the wall.

'You disrespect that lady again,' spat Durant. 'By God—'

'I won't!' gurgled Makin. 'Please . . . let . . . go.'

Durant eased his hold and Makin slumped to his knees, coughing and massaging his squeezed neck.

Durant shook his head. 'Take another glug – that'll sort it. I'll be back here about nine o'clock.'

With that, he stalked out to the baking street.

As light seeped out of the colossal sky, men began to drift in from all sectors of the range. Soon, the quadrangle of ranch house, stabling buildings and the men's living quarters was busy with activity. Kerosene lamps suspended on nails cast their glow about the yard and a scent of cooking drifted out of the open door of the chuck hut. Gradually, their horses tended and settled for the night, the hands gravitated toward the long shack abutting Cookie's kitchen. Here, on benches either side of a trio of trestle tables, they massed twice a day for meals. Steve Doughty and Harry Turner always ate in the ranch house.

Soon, with Cookie having hauled in his stew pots, the long shack was abuzz with talk and the scrape of utensils on plates.

Clem swallowed a mouthful of beef and beans and nodded at Riley. 'We'll be hitting Cooper's Town again tonight?'

Riley nodded. 'I've got a thirst and no mistake.'

Saul Vaughan, a veteran of Liam Doughty's reign, spat, 'Steve should put a stop to your drunken antics; it's not right.'

Riley, his eyes blazing, growled, 'You'll mind your own, feller, unless you want some trouble.'

Vaughan shook his head. 'You've missed early starts enough, Saunders! I'll be asking your pay's docked on account of it.'

Riley slid his pistol out of the holster on his right leg and levelled it at Vaughan. 'I told you to stow your mouth.'

Saul half-rose, his face set to a furious glare. 'Pull a gun on me, would you?'

Another ranch-hand put on restraining hand to Vaughan's arm and Clem Daly eased Riley's Colt down. A moment later, peace restored, Vaughan stalked out.

'Hell, but I ain't sure how long I can hold back,' hissed Riley to Clem. 'There're too many pressing at me.'

'Forget it tonight,' retorted Clem. 'Come on, Riley, we'll hit the Stage and liquor up.'

Riley nodded. He climbed to his feet and sheathed his gun. There was one chunk of beef left on his plate and he eyed in indecisively. He shook his head, grabbed a fork and slammed it down on the piece of meat with all the force he could muster.

CHAPTER SEVEN

Makin rose to his feet as the tallboy clock against the office's back wall inched through 8 p.m. Cooper's Town rocked with noise and the shut door of the jail-house did little to dull it. He expected the usual High S thuggery. Soon – as always happened after they'd downed a few drinks in the Stage – they'd start with that gun tomfoolery.

Makin frowned. It felt like his world had plunged out of control. The murders the night before shook him; ex-marshal John Durant worried him more. Finally, there was the constant terror that Riley 'bloodbath' Saunders engendered.

Still, Makin reasoned, the murder of the drifters would pass out of reference rapidly; the issue of Green Ash was problematic but he'd put the fear of God into Carling and Vernon Glebe. Yes, if either spoke, if either disclosed to Durant about finding his friend Luke Gray's body the ex-Federal might bring in other authorities.

He had to speak to Glebe and Carling again; he

had to warn them to keep their mouths shut. He prayed he'd see them before Durant did.

The sheriff gulped then. He needed to converse with another man as well and the idea of doing that repulsed him. No matter his reservations, he had to tell Riley Saunders.

A moment or two later, a buggy trundled over the ruts of Main Street with Carling at the reins and Vernon perched beside him on the cross-seat. Carling steered the vehicle to the hitching rail close to the saloon and both men alighted.

Makin hurried out. He took the boardwalk steps in a leap and covered the distance at a run. Carling had just secured the horse's reins to the rail and he turned to find himself face-to-face with the sheriff.

'God's teeth,' spat Makin. 'Why're you two so late?'

Carling shrugged. 'Garside's got an order in. We're working through the next few nights.'

A kerosene lamp hung off a nail on one of the boardwalk posts and by its cast-out light, Carling noticed Makin's strained countenance.

'What's up, Sheriff?' baited Carling, his lips widening to a grin. 'Mayor read you the riot act again?'

'You'll soon lose that smirk,' barked Makin. 'Lassiter's took on silver-hair as deputy.'

Carling became stony-faced in an instant. Beside him, Vernon Glebe emitted a loud gasp.

'Now you're seeing it,' snarled Makin. 'What I said before about you keeping your mouths shut, well, it stands and more beside. This John Durant feller used to be a federal marshal in Missouri. You'll both swing if he gets wind that man he seeks died like he did.'

Carling nodded and Vernon's eyes reflected his nervousness.

'God, Frank,' muttered the younger man. 'You shoved your pistol muzzle in that Durant's face and he might take that a reason for settling some.'

Carling looked perplexed. 'I can't reckon it. Like I told you, I roughed that silver-hair easy like.'

'Take it from me,' drawled Makin. 'Durant's a tough son of a bitch and best not to tangle with. You tread light about him and say nothing.'

Carling's mouth shaped to reply but a call halted him.

They turned in unison, watching as Frank's wife Becky, their baby clutched to her chest, approached along the boardwalk.

'Frank,' she cried. 'Elle's not well. She's burning up.'

Carling's eyes burned. 'Get back home!' he roared. 'I told you never to come down here.'

Becky Carling looked desperate. 'Frank,' she screamed. 'This baby's took right sick. We need that doc at New Hertford.'

'You're plumb crazy,' spat Carling. 'Drive twelve miles at this time of night. I ain't got the money for no quack fees.'

'You got it for liquor?' Becky flamed defiantly. 'You should—'

She didn't finish. Carling stepped up the board-walk steps and applied a swingeing slap to his wife's face. The force of the blow threw her head back and she struggled frantically to keep her grip on the baby.

A second later, Carling and Vernon passed through the batwings into the saloon. Makin appraised the sobbing woman before turning back to the jailhouse.

It was just past nine when Durant rose from Ned Slocum's table and slid on his Stetson. Anne's agitation had been clearly apparent during the meal and now, following him out on to the boardwalk, she clutched firmly at his hand.

He drew her to him and growled, 'Steady, woman, I told you I'd be safe.'

'You might be,' she uttered breathlessly. 'But those High S men can't be trusted.'

'I reckon that sheriff is to be trusted less,' he intoned. 'I'll be back at the shack soon as the saloon clears out.'

'That usually isn't till past midnight,' she responded.

'Anne,' he said softly. 'You're not planning to deliver more towels are you?'

She scowled and tried to pull away. He clutched her to him and breathed in deeply. 'I had to do it.'

'You're a goddamn fool,' she spat. 'You turn up in my life and then you end up—'

'Hush,' he reassured. 'There's no life in Cooper's Town. Hell, Anne, the place is like a graveyard and unless someone changes that it'll all just waste away.'

She stepped away and nodded. 'I'll wait up, John;

I'll have coffee on the boil.' She strode to the door and glared back. 'You best be here or by God I'll come searching.'

He doffed his hat. 'Yes, ma'am, you can be certain of it.'

Makin watched the High S crew ride into town. Eight had arrived tonight, Riley and Clem Daly amongst them. The sheriff shuddered; he steeled himself to exit the jail again and begin discourse with a man he despised and feared in equal measure. He put a foot toward the doorway but stopped.

A gun blast sounded – someone discharging a slug skyward at a point further down the street – and Saunders responded instantly. Riley whipped his pistol from its holster and sent two slugs up at those black-coated heavens.

The sheriff gulped and backed toward his desk. Go hang, Riley Saunders. Why risk anything against that unstable bastard. No one would talk so let Durant do his best. That ex-federal wouldn't discover a thing and better to let sleeping dogs lie.

At his desk, Makin reached for the depleted whiskey stock. He filled a shot glass with a trembling pour. He gulped the fiery liquid down. It burned into his guts and he clamped his eyes closed, willing with a curse for his nerve to hold.

Durant tensed as the gunfire began. He'd reached the intersection of Liberty Row and Main Street and instinctively tightened his grip on the carbine. A second later, the sound of muzzle blasts subsiding, he prepared to move. A noise on the boardwalk held him still though. He turned toward the shadows cloaking the boards and detected a protracted sob.

'Who's there?' he barked firmly.

Paltry light illuminated Liberty Row, and when no answer came, Durant pulled matches from his pocket and struck one. As the match head surged to flame, Durant saw a woman holding a baby swathed in a folded blanket.

'Please,' Durant intoned softly as the match flame died. 'I'm the new deputy sheriff in Cooper's Town.'

The woman stepped forward. She descended off the boardwalk where a sliver of moonlight offered just enough for her features to be viewed.

'Ma'am,' said Durant shaking his head. 'I'd reckon I don't need to say that being out at this hourt isn't good for a woman or a child.'

She nodded and then began to weep. 'I know,' she spluttered. 'But I'm worried sick on the little girl.'

A few minutes of explanation and Durant gave out a controlled sigh. He fought the rage that flooded into him and tapped Becky Carling gently on the shoulder.

'You stay here,' he said. 'I'll be back with Frank before you know it.'

'He'll be angry,' she replied fearfully. 'I don't—'

'Don't worry,' returned Durant. 'He won't lay a hand to you ever again.'

He navigated down the centre of the dusty street, striding the few hundred yards to where the Stage reverberated to riotous revelry. Men thronged the boardwalk outside and the noise that emanated from inside the saloon was cacophonous.

Durant glanced across at the jailhouse – its door shut and the burn of the office lamps in the windows masked by closed curtains. Durant's guts knotted: Makin had just walked away from a woman and her sick child. They'd be a reckoning about that as soon as he'd dealt with Carling.

Here, where the boardwalk's lamps, lodged on hooked nails, threw out a wave of illumination, people began to notice the badge pinned to Durant's vest.

'Hell,' one man growled. 'No tin star sticks in.'

Durant ascended the steps and jabbed the carbine's muzzle at the speaker's forehead. 'It does now.'

The man shook his head and lunged a hand up to force Durant back. Durant reacted with speed. He swung the carbine round and slammed its butt full into the other's face. The man howled as the rifle butt fractured his nose. A moment later, slumping to his knees, the man struggled to stem a flow of blood.

The others stayed silent as Durant pushed through the batwings. Inside, the place heaved, barely a space at the long counter and all the tables filled. None in there seemed to have noticed Durant's arrival and he worked his way through the crowd of clientele until he sighted the man he was after.

Near the back of the saloon, Frank Carling and Vernon Glebe shared a bottle of whiskey at a circular table.

Durant reached them in an instant. He propped the carbine against the table's edge before dragging Carling up by his shirtfront and applying the back of his right hand to the woodcutter's face. Carling's head lolled back, and he'd have fallen if Durant had loosened his hold. He didn't. He kept Carling on his feet and next delivered a solid punch to the solar plexus. Carling groaned and his eyes rolled in the sockets.

Now voices began to subside. By the time Durant shook Carling back to semi-consciousness, the saloon had turned eerily quiet.

With his free hand, Durant jabbed a finger at Vernon Glebe. 'This scum Carling ain't gonna be much account driving a buggy.'

Vernon visibly shook. 'I don't rightly—'

'You'll drive Carling, his wife and their sick baby to New Hertford. Then you'll wait there till the doctor's seen to the child.' Durant reached into his vest pocket and produced a twenty-dollar coin. 'That's on loan. Tell Carling, when he'll be able to understand, I'll come for my money. I'll be checking tomorrow how that baby is and I got some questions for you and Carling about my friend at Green Ash.'

Vernon gulped and inched to his feet. He took the coin Durant proffered and shakily placed it into a pocket of his pants.

Durant let go of Carling and he dropped to the saloon floor with a loud smack.

'This creature would rather drink than have his sick baby tended by a physician,' he barked. 'I'm not letting that happen.' He glared at Vernon. 'Now, get shifted!'

Vernon struggled to get Carling up and a couple of men at the counter moved forward to assist. They manhandled Carling toward the batwings but stopped as Durant bellowed out again.

'You tell Carling,' he growled, 'if he lays a finger on Becky again, I'll rip him apart.'

Wide-eyed, Vernon nodded and shot out of the saloon.

Durant blew out his cheeks and took a moment to let his anger subside. He suddenly realized that the saloon's deathly silence continued, and, casting a glance around, he noted a sea of blank faces. Perhaps sixty pairs on eyes drilled into him and he shrugged.

'I'm Deputy Sheriff Durant,' he offered picking up the carbine. 'I'll make all your acquaintances at some point.'

At that, with pensive quiet being maintained, he tapped a finger to the brim of his Stetson and stepped steadily toward the exit. He had business with the scum-useless sheriff of Cooper's Town.

CHAPTER EIGHT

Riley slouched on the wing-backed chair and shook his head.

'Hell, he drawled. 'I don't reckon what I just saw.'

'I know what *I* saw,' spat Tom Leyton. 'That's the drifter me and Steve caught on the range couple of days back.'

Riley fixed Leyton with a steely glare. 'That's the man what wounded Steve?'

Leyton nodded. 'Sure was, Riley. He didn't say nothing about him being law, mind.'

'Christ,' intoned Clem. 'He looks a tough bastard too!' Clem gulped. 'And him saying about that . . . well, you know who I mean?'

Leyton frowned. 'Hell, you heard what that feller said?'

Riley scanned around the saloon. Men had set back to their previous activities – the Stage reverberating with noise again and the antics of the deputy sheriff quickly forgotten as people returned to the fevered pitch of hard drinking.

Now, with men crowding the bar once more and

the slam of glasses and card hands providing an unbroken barrage of sound, a person could talk openly and without fear of having their words overheard.

'Boys,' Riley muttered sourly. 'I can't rightly reason it.' He scratched at his stubble-cloaked chin with a scarred hand. 'What's Makin playing at taking on a deputy, and the same feller what's been asking about Green Ash at that?'

Clem locked Riley with a look that spoke of an inner worry. 'What d'you think?'

Riley shrugged. 'I told you stuff's coming to a head.' He reached for his whiskey glass and drained it. 'You mind those two fellers that deputy was speaking to?'

Clem nodded. 'It was that pair of woodcutters names of Carling and Glebe.' He scowled dismissively. 'They're just a couple of drunkards.'

'That's what I don't reason,' said Riley. 'What the hell do they know about anything?'

'Hey, you're right,' returned Clem. 'Unless. . . .'

'. . . Makin's spoke,' finished Riley.

'That don't make no sense,' protested Tom Leyton. 'Makin stands to swing like all of us. Still, I mean. . . .'

'What is it?' barked Riley.

'Those two fellers,' reasoned Leyton. 'That Carling and Glebe, they're Makin's lackeys. Anyone in town'll tell you that.'

'So Makin blabbed,' growled Clem. 'Goddamn it, we should—'

Riley cut him short with a raised hand. 'Steady, boys,' he said. 'Fact is this new law hasn't got a thing on us . . . yet!

'We go after Carling and Glebe?' suggested Clem. 'They're headed to New Hertford on a buggy. It wouldn't take much to catch 'em and they'll stay quiet for good.'

Riley shook his head. 'This new lawman changes things. We split from here and those folks go missing it might give that deputy summat to chew on.'

Clem nodded. 'So what we gonna do?'

Riley's eyes narrowed. 'I'm not sure yet. I need time to think some. Tonight we'll drink. Tomorrow – well, that could be a whole different thing.'

'We start the war?' hissed Clem.

'No,' said Riley. 'That started the day I was born.'

The buggy had gone, rattling slowly over the ruts of Main Street with Vernon driving. Becky Carling was beside him on the cross-seat; her no-good husband Frank tipped virtually senseless into the back by two fellers from the saloon.

Makin cursed and a moment later, back at the jail-house desk, he grabbed for his whiskey, swallowing the last dregs straight from the bottle. He gasped, that hot slide of pleasure into his guts easing his tension. As his hand brought the bottle away, he heard the door creak open and saw a shadow growing over the office floor.

Durant filled the doorway, his foreboding stature illuminated by the glow of the jail's two kerosene lamps making the sheriff's guts lurch.

'Get rid of that,' growled Durant, 'pick up your gun and we'll do what we're paid for.'

Makin chucked the bottle behind him and it shattered against the back wall. 'Go to hell,' he spat. 'I'm sheriff and I don't get told.'

Durant cocked and levelled the carbine. 'That badge might not mean much to you Makin,' he snarled. 'But it does to me; it should mean summat to the decent folk of Cooper's Town as well.'

Makin shook his head. 'I'm minded in this place,' he snapped back. 'I've survived this long on it.' He sneered now; his eyes alight with contempt and anger. 'You wouldn't use that gun on me, Durant!'

'I wouldn't think twice on it,' said Durant testily. 'Now, get your rifle – you're patrolling with me.'

Makin shook his head and hauled a carbine out of the long cabinet. He remembered Durant's hold on his throat earlier and wasn't keen on a repeat.

'We're patrolling this town back to front,' said Durant as they stepped out on to the boardwalk. Main Street had quietened after the incident in the saloon. 'We'll head back here later.'

Makin shrugged. 'You're headed but one way,' he drawled. 'I already told you that!'

The elaborate hands of the saloon's tallboy clock showed past midnight and the Stage's clientele had thinned. Now, save for the High S men still occupying the raised section's chairs, only a scattering of drinkers remained.

Bert Lewis mused on the night's events. Durant had shown his true colours. A wolf in sheep's clothing sprang to Bert's mind. Mayor Lassiter had been cock-a-hoop when announcing the new deputy's appointment earlier in the day but Bert had doubts. The beating Durant dished out to Frank Carling had dispelled those. Maybe this signified a change for the better. A barkeep shouldn't have to strap on a gun.

Bert threw a quick glance at the High S men and prayed they'd disperse soon. Those murders last night had been the last straw. With any luck, after this bout of drinking, there'd be a burst of gunfire outside and the High S men would gallop out to cross the few miles of prairie to the ranch. Only then could Bert relax. He'd settle to one of the empty tables and take a couple of drinks himself.

Bert buffed a glass and waited as the last of the locals began to gravitate toward the batwings. He noticed the High S men rising from their seats and downing those last dregs of whiskey. Bert sighed and thought longingly of a tall glass of cold beer he would soon quaff.

'Say, Bert.'

The barkeep turned and saw a Cooper's Town resident called William Brady had halted halfway to the exit.

'Yeah, Will, what is it?'

'That new deputy looked a mean son of a bitch!'

The High S men began to descend the steps from the raised section, their spurs scraping the Stage's floor planking as they moved.

Bert shook his head and said sharply, 'Get away home with you, Will. There's a good fellow.'

'But hell,' spat Brady. He'd drunk enough and it had loosed his tongue. 'That deputy sure smacked Frank Carling some; I'd reckon he'll stamp any goddamn thugs out of Cooper's Town.'

Brady felt a force haul him about and he was face-to-face with a snarling Riley Saunders.

'That right, feller,' growled Riley. 'That big ole deputy gonna put a stop to trouble hereabouts?'

Riley drew his Colt and discharged a bullet into the ceiling. The bang of the gun in the confines of the saloon echoed deafeningly, and a moment after, splinters of plaster rained down.

Fear sobered Brady up and his look was panic-stricken. 'I – I never meant . . . it's just—'

Riley clutched at Brady's shirtfront and jabbed the Colt's muzzle at his forehead.

'Stay a bit,' gasped Bert Lewis from behind the bar. 'Will's well in drink, Mr Saunders.'

'I don't give a whore's hell what he's drunk,' raged Riley. 'Just what he's said.'

Brady shook with terror. 'I didn't mean nothing by it; I swear to God I didn't.'

Riley dragged Brady across the saloon – the few locals still there parting to allow a route to the batwings. In no time, Brady was sprawled in the dust of the night street and Riley descended the board-walk steps to join him. By the light thrown from the Stage's lamps, the High S men crowding the batwings saw it all.

'Please,' the kneeling Brady begged. 'I didn't mean nothing by it. My mouth runs off in drink. I got to learn to keep it shut. I will, I promise you that, I will!'

'You called me a thug,' returned Riley icily. 'I just can't let that go.'

The man adopted a praying attitude – hands together and lifted up in supplication and mercy. 'Oh, please God. Oh, please. I don't want to die.'

'None of us wants to die,' baited Riley cruelly. 'Sometimes it's just got to be that way.'

Riley's gun blazed flame and smoke. A second later, the slug from it ripped into the skin of Brady's forehead. The victim held there on his knees a moment – his face as a death mask – before he crashed on to the earth.

There was laughter and clapping from behind and Riley bedded his pistol. He bowed low to his appreciative audience. 'That, fellers,' he boasted, 'is how it's done.'

CHAPTER NINE

Durant, having tired of Makin and patrolling alone now, closed fast on Main Street as that gun blast broke. He sprinted to find a crowd of men outside the saloon. He cocked the carbine, surveying the rough-looking characters either clambering on to horses or descending the boardwalk steps with loud talk and laughter.

Durant took in the crumpled body of a man in the dust. He stepped forward and assessed the bloody hole in the corpse's forehead. A quick search showed no gun in the slain man's hands; no weapon lay on the street nearby either.

Right then, most of the men were in the saddle. Bert Lewis had appeared in the batwings and Durant fixed the barkeep with a penetrating glare.

'Bert,' he demanded. 'How'd this feller die?'

The barkeep shrugged. 'I can't say, Deputy.'

The mounted men gave out laughs and whoops, and a couple loosed slugs into the night sky.

'You're all staying till I find out what happened,'

bellowed Durant. 'Hold them horses. This man's been killed and as far as I can see he weren't armed.'

Clem Daly urged his horse round and drove it straight at Durant causing him to step back.

'You mind you own,' Clem spat. 'Lessen you want trouble.'

Durant dropped the carbine and grabbing hold of one of Clem's legs he dragged down hard and pulled the man off his horse. Clem hit the street's surface with a furious grunt and he struggled to get his hand to the butt of his pistol. Durant, reacting fast, stepped forward and applied the top of his boot to the other's chin. Clem howled, flying on to his back and lying there stunned.

A second man lunged for his gun but Durant's Colt was already to hand.

'Your fingers twitch an inch more I'll blast you to hell.'

The man froze. The others halted their mounts too, all watching and waiting.

'Now,' barked Durant. 'You all stay till I work this out.'

A sudden pounding on the boardwalk signified the sprinted arrival of Sheriff Makin. He glanced around and shook his head as he noticed the slain William Brady.

'God's teeth – how'd that happen?'

'I'm just finding out,' snapped Durant. He stepped forward to the one man who hadn't got into the saddle.

Riley Saunders stretched to the entirety of his five

72

feet eight inches of height and he surveyed the deputy with a stone-faced glare. 'You heard that feller, lawman, you mind your own!'

Durant sighed. 'Give me your gun.'

Riley shook his head. 'You're crazy, mister!'

Durant jabbed his Colt's muzzle into Riley's chest and with his other hand, he quickly slid the High S man's pistol from its holster. He wrapped the barrel of Riley's revolver in his palm and felt the warmth of recently discharged slugs.

He nodded then. 'This gun's been fired.'

'You are crazy,' bellowed Riley. 'You can't prove I shot that man. Who'd the hell you think—'

He didn't finish. Durant dropped Riley's pistol and swinging his own gun round in a fast movement, he brought the revolver's butt down hard across the High S man's head. Riley groaned, swayed a moment before dropping to the street.

Durant sheathed his Colt and dragged up the carbine. A moment later, he'd cocked and levelled the rifle.

'Now,' he yelled. 'This piece of dirt's arrested for shooting up Main Street. The rest of you get out of town or you'll join him.'

Clem had clambered back to his feet and rubbing at his aching chin he growled, 'You just made a big mistake.'

Durant pressed the carbine's muzzle at Clem's throat. 'Just one more word, so help me!'

Clem backed off and was soon in the saddle. A moment later, with a burst of skyward gun blasts, the

High S crew drove their horses out of town.

'Do you realize what you've done,' barked Makin.

'Yeah,' said Durant dragging Riley to his feet. 'I've sent a message.'

'No,' groaned Makin. 'You've signed our death warrants.'

They reined their mounts to a standstill a mile out of Cooper's Town. Here, in the pitch dark enfolds of the grassland vastness, Clem tried to think.

Finally, Tom Leyton broke the quiet. 'What'll we do?'

'I'm not sure,' snapped Clem. 'They can't hold Riley long.'

'The locals won't talk, will they?' returned Tom. 'I mean, what if it's told Riley gunned that feller down?'

'Not a bit,' intoned Clem. 'Them locals know to keep quiet. Like I say, come morning I'd reckon Riley will be headed back to the High S.'

'What if he isn't?' questioned another.

Clem jabbed butt of his pistol. 'Then it's another plan.'

With that, they all raked spurs to their horses' sides and thundered fast toward the High S.

The clock had passed 1 a.m. when Anne got to the jailhouse. She carried a coffee pot and a plate covered in a towel. Durant sat at the desk scribbling down notes on that night's killing, while Makin leant against the office's front wall. He scowled as Anne entered.

'My God,' sneered the sheriff. 'Ain't this nice?'

Durant climbed to his feet and fired a fierce glare at Makin. 'I'd suggest you go home. I'll stand guard for the rest of the night. You take over at eight tomorrow morning.'

'Whatever you say,' scoffed Makin. The sheriff held by the door. 'You can't hold Saunders. There's no evidence against him.'

'Another man's dead,' snapped Durant. 'He's as good a suspect as any.'

Anne gave a gasp. 'Someone's dead?'

'Yeah,' returned Durant sombrely. 'It's a feller name of William Brady.'

Anne shook her head. 'We heard the shooting, of course.' She threw a disdainful look in the sheriff's direction. 'Mind, that's nothing new in Cooper's Town.'

'This Brady,' inquired Durant. 'He's got kin, Anne?'

'Not in town,' she intoned. 'You might reckon that a blessing with the man lying cold. I heard of relations out east.'

Makin built a smoke and blew out grey rings.

'We'd have to send for a judge from Scottsville,' he growled 'That's nigh on eighty miles. I already told you we're at the edge of law out here, Durant. You can't hold Riley in them cells till a judge might turn up.'

'His pistol muzzle was warm,' said Durant truculently. 'That says he fired a shot and it's worth a go.'

'You're the clever one ain't you, Mr Ex-Marshal,'

the sheriff snarled. 'I'm only a hick badge of a back-ward town but I could tell you testing one man's gun isn't evidence. Most of those High S men fired their pistols; all of them could have for what we know. You hold one man's gun and decide he's guilty of murder. No witnesses; no evidence.'

Durant felt despondent. Makin's spat-out words couldn't be argued with. He'd have to release Riley Saunders and hope that a witness would be brave enough to step forward.

'OK,' he barked with annoyance. 'He's released but not till the morning. These High S thugs've got to see I won't stand for it. Holding one of them in the cells overnight just might do it.'

Makin shrugged. 'Fair enough. I won't—'

'No, you won't,' cut in Durant. 'I aim to stay here all night to see Riley Saunders is behind bars until tomorrow.'

Makin shrugged. 'I'll head home for sleep then?'

'Yeah,' drawled Durant. 'You do just that.'

A moment later, tossing his smoke butt on the floor and grinding it with his boot, Makin exited to the boardwalk. They heard his footsteps fade and Anne placed the food on the desk.

'I got worried,' she said. 'I wasn't sure how long you'd—'

He stepped around quickly and embraced her. They kissed passionately and he smiled.

'I couldn't get back,' he said apologetically.

She looked shocked. 'Where's Will Brady now?'

'He's in the cell next to the man that killed him.'

Her brow creased to a frown. 'Something you'll never prove. Oh, John, it's been bad in Cooper's Town these last months and I'm right scared what you're taking on.'

Durant shook his head. 'I can't make this killing stick, Anne, but I won't stop till these thugs are off the streets.'

She shrugged. 'Don't let your food and coffee get cold.'

He sighed and held her tight again. 'Anne, I've got to do this. I've got to send a message to those thugs if this Cooper's Town hell is to end. You do understand, don't you?'

She pulled away and feigned annoyance. 'I'll go home and wait some more, I suppose.'

'I'll be there for breakfast.'

'Just after eight a.m.' she said firmly as she backed to the door.

'Goodnight, Anne,' he said softly. 'Sleep well.'

She shook her head and disappeared into the darkness of Main Street.

Dawn broke as the buggy closed back on Cooper's Town. With darkness dispelled and the sun inching over the distant hills, Vernon sighed with relief. That twenty-four mile return journey across the vast, black prairie had been terrifying. His mind had played a million tricks – each jackrabbit's scratch unimaginable horror waiting to take them.

They'd got back, though. Becky and the baby slept in the rear of the buggy and Frank, silent and brooding, had driven the homeward journey.

Now, as the clapboard profile of Cooper's Town loomed ahead Frank muttered, 'I oughta kill that bastard.'

'Hell's teeth,' Vernon hissed, desperate not to wake Becky. 'He's law isn't he? We seen he's no pushover neither. What's done is done.'

Carling looked as he was about to explode but he controlled his temper. He spat at the underfoot of dry grass and said sombrely, 'God, I need to get away from this place, Vern. I wish I'd never got involved with Makin; I wish we'd never took that goddamn timber out to Green Ash. Mostly, I wish we'd never seen—' He cut off with a half-sob.

'We did, though,' whined Vernon, fighting the bile in his own guts when he recalled it once more. 'And speaking on that what we gonna tell that deputy when he catches up with us?'

Carling fixed Vernon with an inquisitive glare. 'Say, Vern. Now I think on it – why'd the hell Makin pay for that timber?'

Vernon shrugged. 'Sheriff wanted the killing kept quiet? We delivered wood and as far as Garside knows, that Green Ash man paid. That's it. No questions.'

Frank nodded. 'I'd reckon you're right. Maybe he's got money off them High S men to keep quiet too?'

'I can't see Riley Saunders paying no one,' intoned Vernon. 'He'd be more likely just to slit your throat.' Vernon paled then. 'Damn it,' he spluttered. 'Riley were in the Stage when that deputy beat up on you. All would have heard that silver-hair saying he wants a word with us.' Vernon had become frantic. 'Frank,' he said clutching at the other's arm. 'He said he'd speak to us about that sodbuster at Green Ash. Riley and the High S would have heard that.'

'Calm down, damn it,' spat Frank jerking his arm away. 'You'll wake the woman.'

Vernon nodded but he was physically shaking.

Carling fought his own mounting fear as he uttered, 'We'll have to speak to Makin again. He's got to sort this.'

Vernon buried his head in his hands. It would be a bad day. They'd have to drop Becky and the child off at Carling's home and then head straight out to the wood mill for a full day's work. There would be no sleep after the rigours of the night.

The Glebe boy now shared Carling's way of thinking entirely. If it weren't for his elderly father, Vernon would have gotten the hell out of Cooper's Town as soon as he could.

CHAPTER TEN

Durant drowsed in the office chair as Makin walked in. Daylight sat bright in the window, and Durant stifled a yawn. He inched to his feet, each limb aching with tiredness.

'My shift,' snorted Makin.

Durant nodded. 'I reckon so.' He picked up his Stetson and made to leave.

'Say,' Makin called after him. 'I'll give Riley some breakfast and let him loose.'

Durant turned and nodded. 'What about burying Brady?'

'We got an oldster in town who does that. Mayor says a few words on account we ain't got a preacher.' Makin shrugged. 'I'll write it out as killing by person unknown.'

'I'll get witnesses,' said Durant sliding his hat on. 'And when I do I'll hunt that man down like the filthy animal he is.'

Durant disappeared outside and Makin cursed. A few moments later, he stepped through the door to the cell corridor. Riley was perched on the edge of the second cell's bunk.

'You bastard, Makin,' snarled Riley. 'Get me out of here now or you'll be sorry.'

The sheriff, trembling, reached for the keys off a hook on the wall and after a moment of fumbling, he had the cell door open.

'I'm sorry, Riley,' whined Makin. 'It's this feller Durant. Hell, he's trouble right enough.'

Riley pushed through, slapping the sheriff's hat off as he passed, and in no time, he'd positioned himself in the office chair. He pulled out the two drawers and shook his head.

His eyes flared. 'No whiskey?'

Makin shrugged. 'I can brew you some coffee.'

Riley sighed. 'Get your stinking hide over to the saloon and get me some redeye.'

Makin scurried off and ten minutes passed before he returned. Riley spent the time scanning the wanted posters. He and Clem were not part of the panorama of faces and descriptions. He wondered about that as the sheriff bustled in.

'God,' spat Makin. 'That Bert Lewis cut up difficult. He placed a full bottle of whiskey on the table. 'It's all for you.'

Riley uncorked the top and swigged long. He lowered the bottle and sighed. 'That's some good and no mistake.' He pinned Makin with a fierce glare. 'What you done with my mug shot?'

'I burned it,' returned Makin. 'I thought it the best way.'

Riley chuckled. 'You could be on one yourself, Blair boy. Hell, but you're right handy with a knife.'

'Please, Riley,' Makin wailed. 'This is all going wrong. The mayor made me take on that bastard Durant and that ex-federal's on to me about that feller from Green Ash.'

Riley's eyes widened. 'An ex-federal, you say?'

'A marshal from out east,' groaned the sheriff. 'He's like a dog after a goddamn bone. He won't let nothing go.'

'Them two drunkards you have on your shirt tails,' returned Riley. 'Carling, isn't it? Yeah, Carling and Glebe? Why'd he want to talk to them?'

Makin's guts lurched. He couldn't keep it quiet any longer.

'Durant went to Green Ash,' he said sombrely. 'He saw a stack of timber and wants to ask 'em about that.'

Riley shook his head. 'So – why'd you worry?'

'Hell's teeth,' spat the sheriff. 'They found that sodbuster's body!'

Riley's stare was thunderous. 'I told you to get rid!'

Makin wore a worried look. 'I didn't know they'd deliver wood that morning. 'Hell, they got there before I did.' Makin's eyes were wide and fearful. 'That's not all.'

'Say it,' growled Riley.

'They saw you High S boys leaving.'

Riley took another swig from the whiskey bottle and his other hand he slammed in a fist on to the desktop. 'Goddamn, why didn't you say this before?'

'They swore to keep quiet,' bleated Makin. 'They won't say a thing, I promise.'

Riley climbed to his feet. 'Get rid of them.'

Makin felt the room swim. 'Say what?'

Riley got to the door and glared back. 'Get rid of them by tonight, Makin, you hear me?'

With Riley gone, Makin slumped into the seat and grabbed for the whiskey bottle that thankfully Saunders had left on the desk. The sheriff drank several mouthfuls and felt it burn inside.

Blair Makin felt desperate. His life seemed out of control now. He took more whiskey and nodded. He felt like he was in a wagon careering out of control toward a cliff's edge. It could not be too long before everything crashed over into oblivion.

Durant struggled to keep his eyes open. He finished the fine breakfast provided by Anne and despite the copious quantity of coffee he'd consumed, sleep began to overtake him fast. He pushed up out of the seat.

'Anne,' he said croakily. 'I'm as whacked as a man gets. I need a heck of shut-eye.'

She nodded. 'Go. You'll have mapped that nothing happens in Cooper's Town till nightfall. I'll wake you before eight o'clock tonight and you can have your dinner.'

He smiled. 'You're a blessing, Anne, I swear.'

He exited to the street and walked off toward the shack. Twelve hours' blissful sleep awaited and it was worth all the riches in the world right then.

He'd reached most of the way there when a voice hailed him. He turned to see Becky Carling clutching the baby. He doffed his hat. 'Good morning to you.'

She nodded. 'I just came to thank you. My little girl's fine now and Vernon told me you'd paid.'

Durant shrugged but said nothing.

'He also told me what you did to Frank.'

Durant took a deep breath. He expected a volley-fire of condemnation.

'It was the best thing that could have happened.' Becky continued. 'He's learnt a lesson and I thank you for that.'

Durant felt unsure what to say. 'Listen, Mrs Carling, I—'

'He's changed,' she said despondently. 'Summat's happened to make him a different man. I don't know – a year back or so.'

'A year?' said Durant, his interest stirred. 'He ever tell you what?'

She shook her head. 'He won't ever speak on it. Since then Frank and Vernon are always drinking and such like. They used to be so different.' She smiled warmly. 'I'll thank you again, Deputy Durant.'

'You're welcome,' he answered.

She left and he continued to the shack. He locked the door behind him and though he tried to consider the significance of what Becky had just said he was too tired. He crashed on to the bed like a shot man.

Makin stood on the boardwalk as it neared midday.

He watched as Lassiter exited the hardware and crossed the street.

'I heard about that trouble last night.'

'Will Brady was killed,' drawled Makin. 'I've lodged the body in one of the cells.'

'Don't tell me,' spat the mayor. 'High S again?'

Makin shrugged. 'We'd reckon so but it can't be proved right now. Durant said to release Riley till we got witnesses.'

Lassiter nodded. 'I like the cut of this Durant's jib. I'm only getting good reports so far.'

Makin scowled. 'This man Brady – I'll have to bury him on town expense.'

'So be it,' intoned the mayor. 'Where's Durant now?'

'He stayed up all night with the prisoner,' returned Makin. 'He's sleeping some.'

'You'll both be on duty tonight?' queried the mayor.

Makin nodded in reply. 'Sure will. I stayed up with Durant to give him cover and I'm dead on my feet too. I'd reckon to shut the jail for a few hours and get some sleep myself.'

'Do that,' said Lassiter. 'Get home and sleep and you and Durant hit these streets tonight. I got a good feeling all round now.' He headed back to his store and Makin locked the jailhouse door. He walked slowly down the boardwalk to his small house but his mind was racing.

Larry Garside gave an order for the saws to stop at

3 p.m. The whining cutters slowed and died and Carling and Vernon sloped off for a break.

'Wade, Martin,' called out Garside to his two sons. 'We'll go and mark some timber for that Cooper's Town job.'

A moment later, Garside and his two boys headed off into the trees. Carling and Vernon sank thankfully on to one of the wood piles outside.

Right now, mid-afternoon and a sultry heat permeating through the forest floor, they were both glad of the rest.

'Goddamn,' spat Carling swigging water from a canteen. He swallowed some but spat more to the ground. 'Warm,' he growled. 'I'd give my right arm for a cool jug of Stage beer.'

Vernon nodded but the look on his face spoke of a person with greater worries than stale fluid. He'd almost fallen asleep at the blade and the worry of recent events was taking their toll.

'Frank,' he gasped at length. 'What you said last night. We got to get out of Cooper's Town.'

Carling fixed Vernon with a piercing look. 'What money we got to settle somewhere else? We're stuck, Vern. Hell, I wish it was other.'

'That new deputy's a tough son of a bitch,' cried Vernon. 'Maybe we could speak to him.'

'After what he did to me?' spat Carling. 'No, we keep our mouths shut and we'll be OK.'

'You reckon?'

'I'm sure of it, Vern. Trust me – we'll be fine.'

Vernon sighed. 'I hope so. Jeez, I do hope so.'

Carling did his best to smile. 'I'll sleep till next week I reckon. Goddamn it, I don't reckon I've ever been this tired.'

Vernon nodded. 'You're right enough. A few more hours and it's back to Cooper's Town. We'll take a beer in the Stage?'

Carling shrugged. 'Maybe one. I don't reckon to be in the saloon when High S men get in and I need bed more than liquor.'

They climbed to their feet the same moment that a loud bang rent the air. A swathe of birds alighted from the pine boughs with screeching ferocity, and Vernon watched, stunned, as Carling clutched at his chest. A red patch spread over Carling's shirtfront and it was obvious what it was. A second later, Carling slumped to his knees before crashing motionless to ground.

Vernon stared, horrified, at the trees that edged the clearing to his right. He saw someone emerge between the towering trunks. It was someone armed with a rifle and moving steadily towards him. When the man's arm levelled and that gun barked out again, Vernon ran.

He lurched sideways – a slug whipping into the woodpile and kicking up splinters – but a second after he plunged into the trees. He hurtled away, no plan of escape but just tearing between the trunks because his life depended on it. Another ear-splitting explosion followed him and though his lungs burned with the effort, he knew he could not slow.

Soon, he crashed through shrub clumps and briar

barriers that tore at his skin, paying no heed to the pain. He wanted to look back but couldn't bring himself to. He stumbled on, his pace slowing as his body wearied, and then it happened. He screamed out as his foot wedged against an exposed root. A second after, he collapsed to the forest floor, his face slamming into a bed of damp mulch and soil. He groaned and dragged himself back on to his feet. He looked back and gasped with shock and horror. Another gun blast bellowed and he ran again.

'Oh, God,' Vernon screamed out. 'What are you doing?'

He threw himself onward and prayed to survive.

CHAPTER ELEVEN

The afternoon progressed and Riley Saunders slept on. The remainder of the High S crew toiled across the range and Harry Turner seethed at Saunders's idleness. Eventually his fury taking over, Harry resolved to have a go.

Pacing the yard for a while – no sign of Riley's emergence – Harry resolved to challenge a High S man not worthy of the name and definitely not the pay. Saunders had ridden back to the High S ranch compound mid-morning and set straight for the bunkhouse.

They'd been no explanation or apologies.

Finally, his rage at breaking point, Harry stalked into the men's living quarters. He reached Riley's bunk and applied a boot to it. Saunders groaned, the force of Harry's boot sending him rolling off on to the floor.

He'd risen quickly though, his hand lunging for his gun.

Harry drew his own Remington and lodged the

muzzle end against Riley's left eye. 'By God I'll put you out and be glad of it.'

'I tried to like you,' hissed Riley. 'But it's hard. I mean, you with your stuck-up ways living off the spread.'

'Where I live don't got a gnat's business for you,' spat Harry still jabbing the gun into Riley's face. 'Your business is what you get paid for. We ain't paying you to sleep all day.'

Riley grinned. 'We ain't paying? You're a boss now?'

'You don't know the half,' barked Harry. 'Where the hell you been all night?'

'Mind your own,' snarled Riley. 'Or by God, Turner, I'll make you suffer on it.'

Harry cursed and shoved Riley hard, the High S man stumbling back and falling over one of the bunks. He landed in a heap on the floor as Harry turned to exit the hut.

Demented with rage, Riley rose and hauled up his pistol. A second later, he flat-palmed the hammer and the gun spewed flame and smoke as the slug ripped after Turner. Riley cursed as the bullet slammed into the bunkhouse wall as Harry Turner dived through the front door, and then sprinted across the yard.

In the chuck building, Lyle Malone left his pots as the gun blast died out. He waited a moment, unsure. He watched then as Riley staggered out of the bunkhouse toward the corral. In no time, Riley had his pinto saddled and drove the animal fast out through the gallows gate and on to the grassland of the High S range.

Lyle set back to the chuck house when a voice hailed him.

Harry Turner, emerging from a hide site, shouted: 'Lyle, are you with us or against?'

'Mr Turner,' Lyle gasped. 'I'm just the cookie.'

'A war's started,' Harry barked. 'Unless you take a side you're liable to get caught in the middle where it's not safe to be.'

Lyle thought about it. He'd always walked a fine line – garnering the trust of the range-hands and Steve Doughty at the same time. Over the years, this meant he'd been privy to much confidential information. He detested Riley Saunders and his cruel ways and what he'd done to that sodbuster at Green Ash had been beyond sadistic. Over the years, Cookie had seen them come and go from the High S. He'd never known such unstable and unsavoury characters as Riley and his cronies. He made his mind up and nodded frantically.

'I'll get my gun,' he blustered.

'No,' Harry shouted. 'You've got to ride to Cooper's Town and muster what men you can.'

'I'll get my wagon.'

'Take my horse,' roared Harry. 'Just ride fast and get help. We've got to hold the ranch house if we'll keep the brand.'

'You got enough guns to do it?'

Harry nodded. 'I've stocked up over time. There're slugs enough to last if you get a shift to it.'

His mind abuzz, Lyle shuffled toward the corral.

Dusk descended rapidly as the sheriff, sweating profusely, drank whiskey in the jailhouse. Disquiet gnawed at his guts but he knew the end was close. The sheriff locked the door and hauled across the curtains. He headed out back and tore off his clothes. He dragged out a clean set from a cupboard and quickly changed. He glanced out of one of the cell windows to the small pen at the rear of the jail. His buckskin stood there, its head slumped as the animal struggled to recover. Damn nag, Makin cursed; it was getting old and couldn't sustain the pace he'd needed. Now, returning to the front office, he ground his teeth in agitation.

Vernon was still alive. That fool kid had evaded him, and in the background, the Garside men had bellowed out and cried Glebe's name. Finally, fearing the mill owner and his boys were getting too close, Makin navigated back to his horse and rode away. He'd driven the buckskin to its limits, the animal spent when they'd neared Cooper's Town. He's used the alleys then to lodge the horse in the corral at the back of the jail. Luckily, he'd seen no one but that didn't quell his worries. He had to silence Vernon; he had to pray the mill family didn't locate the half-wit first.

A commotion in the street caused Makin to unlock the jailhouse door and step out on to the boardwalk. He watched, tight-lipped as Wade Garside drove his mount in at a gallop firing a pistol into the sky as he did so. The noise began to attract people toward the jailhouse – a large crowd having gathered by the time Wade reined his mount to a standstill.

'Sheriff,' bellowed out the youngest Garside boy. 'There's been a killing at Franklin's Forest!'

Makin shook his head. 'What the hell did you say?'

'Damn it,' bellowed Wade. 'There isn't time. Frank Carling's been shot and lies in the yard. Vernon Glebe's missing. Pa says for you to ride out right now!'

Makin turned to a rapidly swelling crowd and made a dramatic gesture with his hands.

'Sounds like Vernon done the killing,' he gave out loudly.

Above two dozen people had assembled now, and these included Mayor Lassiter and Old Ned Slocum who'd been in the hardware for firewood.

'It's the only thing that makes sense,' Makin bellowed on. 'I'll need a posse to head out and track Vernon down. Those that are willing get your horses and meet me back here as soon as you can. From the sound of it, Vernon Glebe's armed and dangerous.'

'We're not riding a posse,' cried out one man. 'I gotta say, Makin, it's right funny how you're so keen on law and order all of a sudden. You don't do a thing to curb killings on our streets and then want us hunt Vernon down?'

'Yeah,' protested another. 'You've shone your hide on that jailhouse chair too long, Sheriff. Anyhow, I've known Vernon Glebe since he was a babe; that boy wouldn't hurt a fly.'

'But it's got to be Vernon,' whined Makin. 'You all know that fool kid sure enough? Nothing else reasons, do it?'

'I don't give a damn,' returned one of the men in the crowd. 'None of us will hunt down Vernon for you. We need the boy to get back and tell us what happened.'

The crowd started to disperse and Makin turned back to the jailhouse. A hollered voice halted him. He turned to see Lassiter with his arms up.

'Stay,' the mayor yelled. 'We got us Deputy Durant?'

Wade Garside let vent his frustration then. He reined his horse round and drove it back down Main with heels and shouts.

'I can't wait here while you lot argue,' he bellowed 'I got to get to Pa.'

'See, boys?' Makin shouted then. 'We haven't got time. I'll need to ride fast too if I'll catch this killer Glebe.'

Lassiter considered it and acquiesced. 'I reckon you're right on that. I'll bring Durant up to speed and if Vernon does get back the deputy can handle it.'

Shortly after, Makin stepped back toward his office. Ned Slocum minus the kindling he'd set out for, shuffled back toward Liberty Street. He needed to tell Anne straight away. She needed to tell John Durant.

Meanwhile, the sheriff rejoiced. Vernon Glebe would not get back. If it took all night, Makin would hunt Vernon and put him where no one could ask the half-wit a question again.

With his back to those few people still milling on the street, no one saw the sheriff's look of joyous relief. Makin grinned. In the clear now, he could kill again.

In the half-light of the settling evening, Clem watched, curious, as a horse approached fast from the direction of the ranch house. The galloping mustang kicked up dust as it thundered in – its hoofs churning up a layer of parched soil below withering grass blades. At that moment, Clem and a dozen others herded the longhorns toward a field bordering a snaking creek.

As the rider neared, Clem recognized the garb and mounted stature of Riley Saunders.

Clem frowned. He'd heard the gun blast earlier – the boom of the shot carried out from the vicinity of Steve Doughty's palatial residence and the quadrangle. Others mulled upon it at the same time, right then two of Doughty's veteran ropers riding back to check it out.

'Hell, Riley,' Clem muttered under his breath. 'What're you up to now?'

An answer emerged quickly when Riley reined his horse sharply toward those loyal hands tracking back to the ranch house.

A second crack of a discharging muzzle told Clem all he needed to know. The battle for the High S had begun.

The two ropers – Duane Chandler and Claude

Lloyd – both ducked as Riley fired. A slug whipped past Claude's head and he lunged for his pistol. He dug spurs into his mount's sides, driving her at a sweeping pace to outflank Riley. Chandler soon followed, both veterans getting a shot off, but their bullets missing the target. Claude's slug ripped into air; Chandler's landing short, dust spitting up where it bit dirt short of Riley's slowing mustang. The animal reared violently, tipping Riley off its back, the force of the fall hurling the gun from his grip. Those brief moments sufficed. Riley scrambled to his feet, trying to make the distance to his spilled revolver but Chandler and Claude closed on the ranch house road with shouts and kicks.

Riley cursed, grabbing his gun up but his horse was bolting into the distance.

Clem galloped his mount to where Riley stood and barked,'Christ, what goes?'

'Turner's pushed me too far,' spat Riley. 'There's no going back now.'

Clem shook his head. 'There're enough men loyal to Doughty on the range. You sure we got the numbers?'

Riley slid a bullet from his belt into the chamber of his Colt. From all sides men began to ride in, drawn by the rapid exchange of gunfire.

Saul Vaughan hauled his horse still. 'What the hell're you shooting for?'

'Ah, just messing, Saul,' drawled Riley. He gave a disarming grin before levelling the Colt and blasting Vaughan in the chest from close range. Saul cried out, toppling backward off his horse and crashing fatally wounded on the High S grass.

'That's it, sure enough,' growled Clem.

'Heck,' intoned Riley. 'It's cut the numbers some.'

The men galloping in toward Clem and Riley consisted of those they'd recruited – all dubious characters with fraudulent pasts. Leyton led a group of a dozen.

In the distance, a scattering of loyal Doughty cattlemen moved their mounts on to the road and up toward the quadrangle.

'Leyton, get my horse,' growled Riley. 'You other men pin those bastards about the house. No one's getting off the range.'

Leyton dragged his mount round. He urged the sorrel toward the edge of the pasture where Riley's horse now held a stationary vigil. He glanced briefly back to see Clem and the rest of the gang hurtling their mounts up to the house.

Riley, alone with a bruised back and bubbling anger, dusted his range gear and cursed. All had to be swept out in one go – Sheriff Makin, his silver-haired deputy Durant, Carling and Glebe, Steve Doughty and his loyal followers in the ranch house. A night of carnage lay ahead.

CHAPTER TWELVE

Durant, so dead to the world that the gun blast on main hadn't roused him, finally awoke to a persistent rapping on the shack door. He staggered off the bed and hauled back the bolt. A moment later, he saw Anne against a backdrop of the now dark street.

She clasped a lamp by the glow of which he defined her strained features.

'What is it?' he gasped. 'What's happened?'

She stepped in, her head lowered and her body trembling. Finally, fixing him with a pleading stare she sobbed, 'Vernon's killed Frank Carling. God, John, poor Becky will be left alone with that baby.'

Durant shrugged. 'He beats his gal so it won't be a loss.'

She flared at that, her eyes wide and boring into him. 'Did you hear what I said?' she screamed.

She flailed at him with her free hand and he gently held her. She only stopped trying to strike him when he pressed his lips to hers. They kissed intensely again until she pulled back. 'Vernon's killed Carling,' she repeated almost in a whisper now.'

Durant shook his head. 'How'd it happen?'

'I'm not sure. One of the Garside boys rode from Franklin's Forest to tell the sheriff. Seems Frank got shot and Vernon's missing. Makin tried to raise a posse but there isn't a man who'll ride for it.'

Durant's brow furrowed with thought. 'Why'd Vernon do it?'

'Maybe they fell out?' suggested Anne. She realized instantly how ridiculous that sounded. 'Hell,' she spat. 'Of course they fell out, why would any man kill another?'

Durant nodded. 'I'll saddle up.'

Old Ned showed outside the shack then with Lassiter alongside.

'You heard what's happened, Deputy?'

'Yeah,' replied Durant. 'I'll set out there to try—'

'Makin's set to Franklin's,' explained the mayor. 'You'll need to stay in Cooper's Town in case Vernon heads back here.'

Durant shrugged. 'If that's what you want?'

'It is,' responded Lassiter. 'I appreciate both you and the sheriff stayed up all night guarding that High S man and you'll both be beat.'

'What's that, both of us?' growled Durant.

'Yeah,' returned Lassiter. 'Makin told me how you and he sat in the jail till dawn guarding that feller.'

Lassiter moved away and Durant's face took on a look of thunder.

'That lying, no good—' Anne stopped herself from speaking the slur. She shook her head. 'Makin went home to bed; only you stopped all night in the jail.'

'Yeah,' intoned Durant. 'Why'd he say other?'

'He's probably trying to make himself look good with the mayor,' reasoned Anne. 'He didn't want you getting any credit.'

Durant nodded. That made sense.

'Pa,' said Anne nodding at her father. 'You get home. I'll stay here to fix John some coffee.'

She shut the door and sighed. Her body longed for him and he yielded. She put the lamp down and they sank into a passion that blinded the world outside.

Vernon scrambled through the undergrowth half-crazy with fear. People called to him. Those familiar voices: his employee Garside and his eldest boy Martin cried for Vernon to give up.

'We've got two guns here, Glebe. We know you done it. Wade's at Cooper's Town getting the law. Don't be a fool, boy.'

Vernon held still now. He cursed. They wouldn't find Sheriff Blair Makin in Cooper's Town. Even now, that no-good lawman stalked the night-cloaked expanse below these towering trees.

Vernon cursed that sorry excuse for a sheriff named Blair Makin. The Cooper's Town lawman wore a badge of law but he'd slain poor Frank Carling in cold blood. Vernon fought to understand and the death of that Green Ash sodbuster came to mind.

When Vernon tried to rouse himself to action again, fear clouded his thinking so he waited, silent and trembling in the terrifying dark of the forest's interior. He strained his ears to pick up any sound. A few times, birds scratching in the underbrush made his heart jolt. Finally, unable to bear remaining where he was, he moved on once more.

He picked his way forward at a low crouch, inching further into the dark heart of the trees. He'd lie low until the Garsides settled to their living quarters in the mill. With any luck, the buggy and horse would still be outside. If not, it would be a walk to Cooper's Town. Vernon would do it, though. He had to reach Deputy Sheriff John Durant. He had to explain all and hope that silver-hair believed him!

Makin cursed. It had taken time to garner a fresh horse from Old Abel at the livery – his own buckskin broken by that last gallop – and now, as he rode out of town, he listened to pounding hoof falls somewhere ahead. Night sat black and foreboding across the vast prairie but with the aid of the quarter moon's silver slivers, and with his eyes adjusted, Makin saw a rider approach. Whoever it was drove his mount in at a weaving gallop. Makin cursed, reaching for his carbine.

Soon, the stallion beneath him stilled and the rifle levelled, he threw a swift glance backward. The western edge of Cooper's Town showed the orange glow of kerosene lamps and its closeness suggested the noise of a gun blast would carry back.

Makin reined now to intercept the fast approaching rider. Why worry? The lie that Vernon Glebe was a killer was public news. That should suffice. Makin halted his mount again before sighting the rifle for a head shot.

He sighed then. The moonlit view showed it wasn't Vernon thundering in; it was Lyle Malone of the High S. Makin lowered the carbine and waited.

Malone reached the sheriff and reined up hard. 'Hell's teeth,' the ranch cook panted. 'Am I glad to see you? I passed some feller riding like the devil toward Franklin's Forest. I called but the bastard wouldn't stop.'

Makin shrugged. 'Just one of the Garside boys.' The sheriff pushed back the brim of his hat. 'Say, what goes, Lyle?'

'A war's started, Sheriff,' cried Cookie. 'That Riley Saunders shot at Harry Turner. As I rode off the High S, there was a heck of shooting going on. You got to get a posse up and ride back with me.'

'Stay a minute,' barked Makin. 'You sure you haven't been at the cooking sherry?'

'Jeez,' spat Malone. 'I'm telling you the truth, Sheriff. Men might be getting killed back at the ranch and you've got to help!'

'OK,' Makin nodded. 'We'll ride there.'

Malone shook his head. 'You're not rousing a posse?'

'There's no need,' drawled Makin. 'Me and you'll sort it.'

Cookie hauled at his reins and kicked his horse on.

102

'I'm getting a posse,' he roared. 'That's my orders.'

'Malone,' bellowed Makin. He levelled the carbine again and added, 'Goodbye to you.'

A rifle blast cracked out, its echo crossing the distance to Cooper's Town. Two men on Main Street's boardwalk inched out toward the rutted thoroughfare's grass fringe. Another joined them bearing a lamp and a drawn pistol.

'Who's out there?' one yelled.

A strangled cry came back to them.

'It'll be them High S men loosing slugs again,' snapped the man with the lamp. 'I'm not risking my neck out there.'

They headed back to the boardwalk as Lyle Malone lay dying and Sheriff Blair Makin drove his borrowed horse toward Franklin's Forest.

Durant left Anne's embrace as the gun blast sounded.

'Hell,' he muttered. 'They've started early tonight.'

'Don't go,' she pleaded. 'Stay a while.'

He moved off the bed and began to dress. 'I can't, Anne. It's those goddamn High S men again.'

She leant on one elbow and watched him until he strapped on his gunbelt. As he adjusted his Colt, she slid from between the sheets and wrapped them about her as he eased the shack door open.

'Be careful,' she said. 'I *think* I love you.'

He frowned. 'I'm not happy with that.'

103

She looked pained. 'Why so?'

He smiled. 'Because, missy, I damn well *know* I love you.'

A moment later, he sprinted along Liberty and had soon progressed into the town's main thoroughfare. A few men stood on the boardwalk, one with a gun drawn.

Durant jabbed a finger. 'You fired off a slug, feller?'

The man shook his head. 'We heard rifle fire out of town; I'd reckon it's close by too.'

Durant clutched his Colt tightly. 'I'll take a look. You fellers back me up.'

'No way,' retorted another. 'It's them High S boys. You go out there they'll more than likely blast you.'

Durant shook his head and grabbed a lamp from its hooked-nail in one of the boardwalk's awning posts. He strode out, the lamp's glow swaying as he moved until something caught his attention. He gazed down at the badly wounded man and then yelled back, 'I got a hurt man out here. I need help to carry him in.'

Moments later, footsteps pounded as two men joined him at a run. One knelt down and muttered, 'It's Lyle Malone. He's Cookie at the High S.'

'But hell,' spat Durant. 'How in God's name—'

Malone's eyes flickered open and he clutched at the shirt of the kneeling local.

'What is it, Lyle? Who shot you like this?'

'Sheriff,' gasped Cookie. 'Sheriff's shot me.'

'Hell's teeth!' exclaimed the local. 'That right,

Lyle? Are you saying Makin blasted you?'

Malone nodded and then spluttered blood. 'Help . . . at . . . High S.'

Durant knelt himself now. 'Mr Malone,' he said softly. 'What d'you mean, help at the High S?'

'War,' groaned Cookie. 'War's started!' His eyes rolled up and he died there on the prairie.

They lost no time lifting Cookie's body and lugging it back into Cooper's Town. Before long, with Malone's corpse laid out in the street, other people appeared.

Mayor Lassiter stepped forward and looked desperately at Durant. 'What the hell happened?'

'Makin blasted Cookie,' growled one of the men who'd help carry Malone's corpse in from the grassland. 'That no good sheriff's a murderer.'

'Now, stay a bit,' said Lassiter. 'We haven't got proof. Did anyone see it?'

'It was Malone's last words,' said Durant sourly. 'He told us Makin was responsible.'

'You reckon it was an accident?' returned the mayor pensively. 'Maybe he mistook Malone for Vernon Glebe? It could happen in the dark when a man's all tensed up, like.'

Durant shrugged. 'Why didn't he stop and tend to Malone?'

Lassiter nodded. 'Yeah, that sure don't seem right.'

'I'm headed to Franklin's Forest,' said Durant. 'I aim to find Vernon Glebe.'

'Bring that boy back alive,' drawled Lassiter. 'He'll

be brought for trial on the murder of Frank Carling.'

'Oh, I intend to,' returned Durant. 'I need some answers from that boy about my friend Luke Gray.'

Durant dropped the lamp and stepped towards the livery.

'What about Makin?' Lassiter yelled out.

Durant shrugged. 'He'll be arrested too.'

Lassiter sighed. 'I'll send for the judge in the morning.'

Durant didn't answer. 'I've a feeling,' he muttered just out of earshot and tapping the butt of his re-holstered Colt, 'there's only one jurisdiction that matters now!'

CHAPTER THIRTEEN

In the High S ranch house Harry peered through a shattered window to see dark forms scurrying around the yard. He backed away as a double slug blast cleared the frame of more glass and pressing himself against the wall, he slid another cartridge into his carbine.

'They've gotten us surrounded,' he called out. 'Still, I'd reckon Cookie should be at Cooper's Town by now and if we can hold out a couple of hours we'll have help here.'

Steve shook his head. 'You reckon? We'll hold out, I mean?'

'I am not letting that scum get in here without a fight,' barked back Harry. 'Now, kid, find yourself a shooting space and keep blasting.'

Steve nodded, resolved to do whatever Turner told him from now on. He slunk across the room and reached a front window. He looked out then ducked sharply as a slug whistled past his head.

A voice hailed loudly, 'I almost got you there, boy!'

Riley Saunders chuckled as he perched behind a rain barrel by the corral.

'You'll all swing for this,' Steve screamed. 'We sent us a man to Cooper's Town. Sheriff will be on his way here now!'

A burst of laughter answered.

'That sheriff won't do you no good,' bellowed Riley. 'That waste of space is with us. There ain't no help coming. Besides, I reckon you oughta recall favours we done you.'

Harry shook his head, motioning for Steve to stay quiet. Angered, though, nothing could silence Steve right now.

'You got those farms right enough,' screamed the young ranch boss. 'That's about it!'

'That Green Ash feller were a tough deal,' yelled Clem Daly. 'You seen how he'd held out. He wouldn't sign till we cut his ears off. That did it – after that he signed right enough.'

Steve paled and slumped to the floor. He shook his head. 'You killed that man, Riley?'

'Sure we did, boy,' Riley yelled. 'You're getting the same unless you sign over the High S and bring the papers to me. Once that's done, we'll let you all ride out.'

Harry rushed to Steve's window and sent a slug in Riley's direction.

'Go to hell, Saunders,' bellowed the veteran rancher. 'We hold here till back-up comes.'

'It ain't coming,' sneered Riley. 'That sheriff – well, he were part of it. He bloodied his knife like the

108

rest of us.'

Harry shook his head. That claim was too incredible to accept. Riley implicated the sheriff's direct involvement in murder. 'You're lying,' he spat.

'It's true enough,' returned Riley. 'You want to know where I was all night? Well, that goddamn deputy banged me in those cells.' Silence followed a moment then until Riley growled, 'Between you and that silver-hair, Turner, you've pressed me enough. Time's arrived and it ends this night.'

'Go to hell,' Harry offered with venom to his words. He sank down beside Steve Doughty then shook his head. 'I'd say Saunders was lying,' he said sourly.

'What if he isn't?' returned Steve. 'What'll we do then?'

'The only thing we can do,' growled Harry. 'Shoot straight and pray for a miracle!'

Durant heard the gun blasts a distance out. Now, at the forest's eastern edge, he calmed his mustang and secured the leathers. Inside the forest, with night and the massed trees offering nothing but an indeterminable distance of perturbing dark, he inched forward, his Colt drawn.

Makin's maddened voice carried its spat words. 'Come on, Glebe, I know you're still in here somewhere. Come to Sheriff, Vernon, I got a gift for you.'

Another bang broke through the towering ranks of pines, the canopy exploding into its own noise as birds took panicked flight. When all had settled

109

again, Durant navigated on.

Then he stopped. An orange glow drew him to the left. A hundred yards or so further on, he peered into a clearing and saw the illuminated main bay of the wood mill. Three armed men stood in the entrance, one brandishing a shotgun whilst the others held Winchesters.

A sudden crashing in the nearby undergrowth made Durant prime the Colt. A second later, a figure bolted from out of the trees and hurtled across the clearing. Durant dropped to one knee and extended his firing arm.

He did not shoot, though. Another figure showed and Makin's voice bellowed, 'Stop, Glebe. It's over.'

The sheriff strode purposefully out of the fringe of trees at the far end of the clearing. Vernon had frozen near the mill entrance and the sheriff had his carbine to hand and cocked the rifle as he approached. He pointed the gun first at Vernon and then at the three men in the mill doorway.

'I'm taking this half-wit in for murder,' Makin barked.

'I didn't kill anybody,' screamed Vernon. He looked pleadingly at Garside and his sons. 'You got to believe me. It was Makin what shot Frank.'

The sheriff laughed. 'That's a desperate tale, ain't it?'

'You killed Frank!' howled Vernon. 'Lie as much as you want, nothing won't change that. Please, Mr Garside,' wailed Vernon. 'Don't let him take me. He'll kill me too.'

'They'll be no help for a murdering pig like you, Vernon,' Makin said. 'You got to face what's due.'

Durant stepped into the open and said firmly, 'And so, Sheriff, have you.'

Makin spun round. 'God alive,' he spat. 'How the hell—'

'Yeah,' drawled Durant. 'You thought I'd be back in Cooper's Town while you murdered this boy. I said murder, Makin. You know, how you blasted Lyle Malone back on the prairie there?'

'Cookie's dead?' Garside exclaimed. 'Hell, I've known Lyle nigh on twenty years.'

'Shot down like a dog,' Durant pressed on. 'Cookie was another innocent man slain by this here so-called sheriff.'

'That was an accident,' retorted Makin. 'It can happen in the dark. I thought it was Vernon coming to kill me.'

'Well,' intoned Durant. 'That's for a judge to decide. I'm taking you in, Makin, for murder of Lyle Malone and Frank Carling.'

The sheriff jabbed the carbine at Durant. 'Get back,' he spat. 'You been pushing at me since you hit town and I ain't taking it no more. You should have rode on through, Durant. Now you'll suffer on it.'

A loud click caught Makin's attention and he glanced across to see all the Garside men with their guns primed.

'Now just back off,' screamed Makin. 'This ain't right.'

'What isn't right is you wearing that badge,'

111

snarled Durant. 'You're a killer and a no-good and you'll stand trial for it like I said.'

Makin started to back away, the jerky action of his rifle suggesting he was panic-stricken. He directed the muzzle first one way then the next, never settling on a potential victim for more than a moment.

'Give it up,' said Durant. 'If you run I'll hunt you down.'

'Get to hell,' spat Makin. A burst of flame from the carbine sent Durant diving for the ground. A slug sped over his prone form and a moment after he was back on his feet to see Makin plunging beyond the tree-line.

Durant approached Vernon and the young man began to sob.

'I'm telling the truth, Mr Durant,' Vernon wailed. 'Sheriff killed Frank.'

Durant nodded. 'I believe it, boy. Just tell me why.'

Vernon hesitated. 'It was on account of that feller at Green Ash.' Vernon shoved a fist into his own mouth. A moment later he removed his hand and gasped, 'All on account of that me and Frank found the body.'

Durant's world swam. He'd never fainted before, but when his head settled again a moment or two later, he reckoned that was as close at it got. Rage and desperate hurt flooded through each vein.

'We delivered a timber order,' Vernon persisted. 'We found that man and then, well. . . . Hell, I don't want to say no more.'

Garside shook his head. 'That can't be right. I got

paid for that Green Ash order.'

'Makin,' howled Vernon. 'He gave Frank the money to make sure no questions got asked.'

Durant battled a surge of emotion as he uttered, 'Luke Gray was my friend. What happened?'

Vernon battled those inner demons but eventually blurted out the full facts. Afterwards, he muttered, 'We buried him proper, like. Your friend is here in the forest.'

Durant turned and strode in the direction Makin had fled.

'Deputy Durant!'

He stopped and looked back.

'You do believe me, don't you?'

'Yeah, Vernon,' returned Durant. 'I guess I do.'

'Then you best know it was the High S that killed your friend. It was Riley Saunders.'

Seeking revenge, Durant hurtled between the trees.

The clock ticked on and tiredness began to overtake them. Harry Turner climbed to his feet and grabbing a jug of water, he tipped it into a bowl and splashed his face liberally.

'We got to stay awake,' he muttered. 'Get some coffee on or summat.'

'I wish Cookie was here,' returned Chandler. 'He'd have it brewed right enough.'

'He should have been back by now,' groaned Claude Lloyd. 'Summat's got to have happened.'

The four of them still held post in the front room

of the ranch house. The other six men Harry had stationed about the ground floor. There'd been no gunfire for a time now.

'You reckon they'll be as tired as us?' implored Claude. 'God, but I could sleep some.'

'We'll do shifts,' said Harry. 'A couple sleep at a time.'

Claude nodded, praying he'd get his head down first.

Dane Chandler grinned. 'I'd reckon as—'

He didn't finish. Shattering glass preceded a fireball that swept across the room as hurled in kerosene lamps exploded over the floor. A sheet of flame drove them all to their feet and towards the door. Out in the hallway, all of them coughing from the acrid smoke, they took stock.

Harry shook his head. 'I'm going back in.'

'What're you doing?' Chandler spat. 'You'll be burned else choked to death.'

'I got to,' spluttered Harry. 'We got to get the shutters closed and those flames out.'

Quickly then, they all moved back into the room, holding their breath and stamping where the fire bit into the wood floor. Soon, Harry had slammed the internal shutters and drove the wood bolts across. At last, the last flames subdued, they all retreated into the hallway again.

'What about the smoke?' Steve gasped. 'We'll all be choked unless we can clear it some.'

Harry held a handkerchief over his nose. 'Those shutters's got firing holes in them. With those

114

windows blasted out that smoke'll soon get drawn out.'

It happened as Harry predicted and before long they re-entered the front room. Ironically, by dint of one of the still shining wall lamps, the damage was clear to see: floorboards scorched black in places and an expensive rug left as a charred ruin.

Steve got to his knees and scuttled toward the window. He examined the shutters – not having seen them closed since his childhood days. He'd forgotten about the rifle muzzle holes that allowed defenders inside to shoot out. As Steve knelt there, he felt a cooling breeze drift in through the holes and this had dissipated the choking smoke.

'When we started up here Indians still rode this land,' said Harry then. 'They had a shine for fire arrows so those inside shutters were needed.' Harry fixed them all with a fierce glare. 'Still, those shutters are wood and they won't stop a slug so be careful. We'll need to get round the house and secure all the windows.'

Men quickly scattered and some time had passed before they all gathered again in a smaller drawing room.

'They won't throw lamps in again,' growled Harry. 'That's one relief.'

'Hell,' groaned Claude. 'Trouble is we can't use those shooting holes. We stand up to get a sighting we're likely to get blasted.'

'We are not likely to hit anything if we could,' said Harry. 'They'll be well hidden about the yard. It's a waiting game now.'

'We got to hope Cookie's coming with help,' sighed Chandler.

Harry shook his head. 'There isn't any help coming.'

'What?' Steve gasped. 'But Cookie's gone—'

'Who's he gonna tell at Cooper's Town?' returned Harry.

'That goddamn sheriff that's who,' intoned Claude Lloyd. 'And from what Riley says that there badge is up to his neck in crime.' Claude shook his head. 'We're on our own, boys.'

'I don't get it,' said Steve to Harry. 'You said it was a waiting game. What the hell we waiting for, then?'

Harry didn't answer. There was no need. The grim look on his face said it all.

CHAPTER FOURTEEN

Bert Lewis poured beers for the men now crowded into the saloon. The place buzzed with noise – people chattering in groups. Mayor Lassiter, struggling to make himself heard, resorted to climbing on a chair and waving his arms desperately.

Bert followed the town official's efforts and finally, stepping away from the beer pump, he picked up his shotgun. He sighed, imagining the new damage. The scars of Riley Saunders' gun blast the day before showed vividly on the ceiling.

When the shot came, it quelled the talking instantly. The 12 bore, roaring its blast in the confines of the bar, drove men to their knees as one. It took time for people to get to their feet again, some still cowering beneath tables until others tempted them out.

Lassiter, his clothes coated by plaster dust, nodded

at the barkeep. He gestured at the collective citizenry then.

'Men,' he bellowed. 'This is the size of it: we got Lyle Malone and Frank Carling dead. From what's been said, Sheriff Makin killed Lyle; we haven't got proof on who killed Frank Carling.'

'I heard Vernon Glebe done it,' called out one man.

'Till we speak to Vernon,' said Lassiter, 'it's not proved.'

'I was in Main Street when that Garside boy rode in,' added another. 'Sheriff said Vernon did it. I heard it plain.'

'About that sheriff,' a third man added. 'Where the hell was he when Frank Carling got killed?'

The question shocked some but others had long had suspicions about the lazy, untrustworthy sheriff of Cooper's Town. A murmur went up.

'Men, men!' bellowed Lassiter. 'This is darn crazy. I know for a fact that the sheriff were at his house most the day. He slept on account of guarding a High S feller all night.'

A high-pitched voice cut in, 'That's not true.'

All heads swung at the same time to see Anne Slocum and her father Ned pushing through the batwings.

'We heard about this meeting,' added Anne. 'So me and Pa come down to put our bit in.'

'Go on, Anne,' said Lassiter. 'What weren't true?'

'The sheriff didn't stay up with John Durant,' barked back Anne. 'Hell, Makin set to bed just past

1 a.m.'

'Durant tell you that, Annie?' queried Bert Lewis.

'No,' answered Anne firmly. 'I was at the jail when Makin left for the night.'

A gasp escaped many mouths and Old Ned surveyed his daughter with a look of shock.

'Hell, gal!' he spluttered. 'What was you doing round the jail that time?'

'I took John coffee and such,' said Anne. 'I am old enough, Pa!' She fixed Lassiter with a fierce stare. 'Fact is, Mayor, Sheriff Makin lied; he didn't stay up guarding the prisoner. A man that can tell that lie's capable of a hell of a lot more.'

'You hear what you're all saying?' exclaimed Lassiter. 'You suggesting the sheriff had summat to do with Frank's killing.'

Abel Field pushed himself forward.

'I ain't never liked nor trusted Makin,' growled Abel. 'So when that sheriff came for one of my horses this evening I couldn't rightly reckon it. I mean, him having that buckskin and all.'

Lassiter shrugged. 'Maybe his buckskin's lame. That don't mean a thing.'

'I got round the back of the jail,' said Abel. 'I took a look at that buckskin. I was curious, like. That poor beast's lame all right. It'll never be much use again. It's been darn run to its end and it's been rode there today.'

A murmur erupted again but this time Lassiter's raised arm quelled it.

'This is still just guessing but there's enough suspicion I'd reckon,' said the mayor. 'We got Vernon Glebe out at Franklin's Forest with Makin hunting him. We got Deputy Durant hunting them both. We also got trouble out at the High S.'

Bert Lewis shrugged. 'What're you suggestin', Mayor?'

'I know how folks feel. We all been scared these last months but I reckon time's come when we stand up and fight back.'

'I'll ride,' shouted one local.

'I will too,' bellowed another.

Lassiter nodded. 'As many as willing get your horses and guns and meet back here soon as you can.'

Men dispersed quickly and as the saloon began to empty, Anne sank into a seat. Old Ned approached the bar.

'What'll you have, Mr Slocum?' asked Bert.

'Two brandies,' returned Old Ned. 'It's been some shocking news right enough.'

'Don't shoot! Don't shoot! It's me, Sheriff Makin.'

Soon, a horse's hooffalls clattered along the stone-flecked lane leading up to the High S yard and the murky shape of a mounted man appeared. Tom Leyton leapt up and grabbed the reins as the sheriff neared and a second later Makin slid, panting, out of the saddle.

'Goddamn it, Makin,' spat Riley. 'What're you doing here?'

'It's all blown,' screamed Makin. 'I killed Lyle

Malone; I killed Carling but the Glebe boy's got away. That stinking scum Durant's after me.'

Riley rose and approached the near hysterical lawman.

'That right?' he drawled.

Makin nodded and shaped his lips to speak but a smashed fist to his face sent him to his knees. He slumped to the ground and Riley brought another fist down into the small of the sheriff's back. Makin lay sprawled face down in the night dust.

'Goddamn piece of dirt,' snarled Riley. 'I'm not losing it all on account of you.'

'Durant's headed here,' called out Clem. 'What you reckon?'

'He's but one man isn't he?' growled Riley. 'Besides, me and that silver-hair have got business to settle.'

Clem shrugged. 'We got to split tonight; there's no way we'll have safe necks after this.'

Riley, enraged, bellowed at the shuttered-up ranch house. 'You hear that, you men in there? Cookie's dead. No help is coming your way this night. Better to give up and sign them deeds over. I give my word no man among you will be touched.'

One of the shutters flew open and Harry Turner's voice roared, 'Go to hell, Saunders. There isn't a thing you can do. You won't get in this house and we'll sit tight a while.'

Riley cursed and kicked out at Sheriff Makin's still prone form. Riley's boot landed with a thud and Makin howled. A moment later, dragging a knife from his belt, Riley applied it to Makin's throat.

'I'll cut this lawman in strips,' he cried at the house. 'You'll hear him scream like nothing you've heard before.'

'Like he cut that sodbuster at Green Ash?' shouted Harry. 'Be our guest; it'll be a sound we all want to hear.'

'Please,' Makin whimpered. 'Don't cut me like that, Riley.'

Riley jerked his knife away and Makin pressed himself into the dust with a whimper. He lay there, trembling and praying.

'No,' Riley bellowed. 'I won't cut this sheriff. Soon as we've dealt with Durant, we'll ride to Cooper's Town. We'll cut us some other folks.' Riley snickered. 'Yeah, you live in Cooper's Town, Turner! I hear you got yourself a plump apple-pie wife in that there town.'

'You scum bastard!' screamed Harry Turner.

'Yeah,' baited Riley some more. 'We'll cut us Turner's fat whore wife after maybe having some fun with her first.'

A gun blast flashed out of the ranch house window and Riley ducked, laughing loud. He stayed hidden in the shadows and muttered, 'Just a pity this deputy ain't got someone in town.'

'He has.'

Riley scuttled across to Makin and shoved the knife at the sheriff's ear. 'Say what, mister?'

'Durant,' rasped Makin, desperate to pacify Riley. 'He's got him a fancy piece in Cooper's Town. It's a girl name of Anne Slocum.'

'Well,' drawled Riley. 'If we can't get to the mountain, we'll make the mountain come to us.' He rose to his full height despite the danger. 'Mount up, boys,' he roared. 'We ride to Cooper's Town to get us some fun. I want a few men to stay here to keep these dogs' heads down a while.' He dragged Makin to his feet and thrust the knife blade at the sheriff's face. 'You're coming too, law pig!'

Inside the ranch house, Harry slumped to his knees and buried his head in his hands.

'So help me,' he howled. 'I'll make the man suffer.'

All the blood had drained from Steve's face. 'God,' he spat. 'What do we do?'

'Right now,' returned Dane Chandler, 'not a thing we can do. When Riley and the main group leave we'll storm the others.' Dane moved across and put a reassuring hand on Turner's shoulder. 'It'll be fine, Harry. We'll sort this out.'

Harry looked up with a look of despair. 'We've got to, Dane. Anything happens to Clara I won't be able to live another day.'

CHAPTER FIFTEEN

Durant urged the mustang into the black distance of the vast prairie. He rode blind, hurtling the horse across those unknown miles. At times, though, slivers of moonlight struck at white painted signs that warned people of the dangers of crossing High S land.

He drove the stallion on, devouring those acres and willing Steve Doughty's ranch house to rise out the dark horizon with glowing lamps to show him the way. A sobering thought came to him then: a range this size in the depth of night and you could ride in any direction and miss what you sought. He pushed on and just hoped.

He gritted his teeth as he thought about Sheriff Makin. Somewhere ahead, desperately seeking a way out, Makin would head to Riley Saunders. Riley and the sheriff had both participated in the killing of Luke Gray and Durant knew that Makin would seek protection and solace from the murderous other.

A sudden noise made him rein up sharply. He

grabbed for his carbine, ears straining to identify the sound. A second later, hoofs pounding fast behind, he cocked the rifle and readied to fire. A shout made him lower his guard.

'It's us, Deputy,' a voice cried. 'Wait up!'

Durant shook his head as four horses thundered into view.

'Hell's teeth,' he spat. 'What're you doing?'

'We're helping out,' returned Vernon Glebe. The young man gave a curse. 'I owe somebody,' he growled. 'That stinking no-good sheriff I'd reckon. Me and Frank shouldn't have kept quiet like we did.'

'Vernon,' intoned Durant. 'Who could you tell?'

'Till you touched town, likely no one,' said Vernon. He held up a rifle. 'Mister Garside gave me this. They call me a half-wit but I can shoot straight enough.'

Durant nodded. 'You've all got guns?'

'Sure have,' hailed Garside. 'I'm along on account of Cookie. A good man was Lyle Malone. I reckon folks got to back decent law when the time comes.'

'If you're sure,' growled Durant. 'It'll be risky.'

'We're not soft in the head,' retorted Garside. 'Anyhow, we're five now which is a darn sight better than one in my counting. Hell, Mr Durant, who you reckon you are, the whole goddamn law business wrapped in one?'

Durant grinned. 'I reckon I need yanking back now and then.'

'You got us now,' said Garside. 'We'll back you up.'

Durant nodded. 'You mind where the ranch house is?'

Garside jabbed the 12 bore's barrel to their west. 'You were riding in the plumb wrong direction, Mr Durant. Follow me and I'll get you there.'

They raked spurs to their horses and plunged into the night.

Riley and his crew departed with a clattering of their horses' hoofs across the yard.

When all fell quiet outside, in the ranch house Harry checked both his rifle and the Remington strapped at his hip, before he glanced expectantly at the others.

'We're all set,' muttered Claude Lloyd. 'Three of us go out the front; three more out of the sides; the rest to head out the back.'

Harry nodded. 'I'll take the front and—'

'I'll be with you,' cut in Steve.

'And me too,' added Dane Chandler.

Harry shrugged. 'We go out fast and firing. That way we might have half a chance.'

Steve frowned, his features pinched with worry. 'How many you reckon they got out there still?'

Harry patted Steve's shoulder. 'Hardly any I'd reckon. Besides, you're snake-skinny and look at my gut. You'll be fine.'

Steve tried to smile. He knew Harry suffered given the risk to his wife; the big man showed little of that right now.

'OK,' said Harry. 'We set to our posts and I'll fire a shot as a signal. Then it's out fast.'

They split up, Harry, Steve and Chandler making

their way to the front door. Harry muttered constantly as he checked and re-checked his pistol.

'It's loaded, Harry,' hissed Chandler. 'That chamber were stacked when you last checked it and it still is now.'

Harry nodded. 'I know, Dane. It's just something to do.' He pinned Steve with a protective stare. 'You ready, boy?'

Steve gripped the butt of his Colt and took a deep breath. 'Yeah,' he intoned. 'Ready as I'll ever be.

'Hey,' returned Harry. 'You recall what your pa always said when we were in a tight fix?'

Steve did. He remembered those times, as a boy, he'd seen his father ride out at the head of his ranch-hands to quell Indian raids or the attentions of bandits as Liam struggled to establish the High S in hostile country.

Steve smiled. 'I'd reckon it's fitting, right enough!'

Harry raised his revolver, finger tensing at the trigger. 'We say it now?'

'Yeah,' drawled Steve. He watched Harry's trigger finger flex and he opened his lungs. He ached for his pa as he screamed in unison with the others, 'For hell and the High S. . . !'

'Anne? Mr Slocum?'

They both turned in their seats to see Clara Turner stepping tentatively through the Stage's batwings. She wrapped a blue shawl tightly around her shoulders; her face looked drained.

Anne rose quickly and ushered Clara to a seat.

'Bert,' Anne called, 'a brandy for Clara.'

The drink delivered, Clara sipped it with trembling hands.

'I heard there's trouble at the High S,' she said lowering the glass. 'I'm worried sick about Harry.'

'I won't lie,' answered Anne. 'Something's happening for sure. But John Durant's out there and I reckon he'll do what he can.'

Clara shook her head. 'John Durant?'

'Our new deputy,' responded Old Ned. 'I joked with him about Anne making a good wife!'

'Hush, Pa,' chided Anne. 'Me and John are just friends.'

'Coffee at 1 a.m. friends,' snapped Old Ned. 'I weren't born yesterday, my gal. I got eyes and ears.'

Clara gave a sob and it stopped their playful banter. 'I heard say Lyle got killed.'

Anne nodded. 'Cookie's dead, Clara. But like I say, I'm sure Harry will be fine.'

'I told him to give it up,' ranted Clara. 'When Liam Doughty passed on I told him to leave. He just insisted; he kept saying he had to help young Steve same as he helped his pa. Why didn't the big fool listen to me?'

When tears came, streaming down Clara's face, Anne dried them and put a comforting hand to the older woman's arm.

'Now, hush, Clara,' she said. 'Drink your brandy – it'll make you feel better.' Anne sighed. 'After, we'd best break the news to poor Becky Carling.'

*

They galloped on, hurtling their mounts across the flatland expanse of night-clothed land. The moon, a luminous curve of deepest silver cast hints in the distance – clumps of trees, a course of water, a cattle herd unsettled and scattering from the drumming intensity of their horses' hoofs.

Then, rising out of nothingness, appeared the faintest glow of structures. A scattering of yellow sat in the distance – perhaps a kerosene lamp on a hooked nail, or maybe a part-curtained window's outlook of light.

'The High S,' bellowed Garside. 'Get ready, boys!'

Durant dragged out his Colt and gripped it as he rode. He'd vowed to bring Makin in alive but his hatred of the crooked sheriff had peaked to a point of absolute rage. The way Durant felt at that moment, the chance of Makin still being alive at dawn was a slim one indeed.

Suddenly, all had changed. A mass of movement made them all rein to a halt. A confusion of shapes emerged from the direction of the ranch.

'God,' spat Garside. 'It's riders headed out.'

'You reckon Makin's with 'em?' added Wade.

'Hell knows,' Garside retorted. 'Only way we'll—'

A gun muzzle spewing flame cut him short. The slug barked out its passage, and they all ducked as the bullet whistled past in the chilling air.

'They're moving our way,' cried Garside. 'This is it!'

The riders exiting the High S turned sharply and galloped in. Guns sparked, bullets scything the air and missing by inches.

Durant levelled the Colt and tried to define a target. Seeing one at last, he pressed the trigger and the pistol jerked and blazed. A slug left the muzzle to a flash of fire and an instant later a shape crumpled to earth with a strangled cry.

A clear, loud bang sounded from Garside's shotgun then. Slug blasts from Wade and Vernon rapidly followed.

More bullets returned followed by a desperate wail from Martin Garside. The young man slid off his horse and hit the earth with a loud groan.

Durant got off a couple more shots, as did Wade and Vernon, and suddenly, to all their relief, the mass of approaching riders reined away.

'They're turning,' yelled Vernon. 'They're set to town.'

A few moments passed, the drumming of the departing riders fading, before Garside flew off his horse to attend to his youngest boy. Thankfully, despite a wound to his shoulder, Martin would live. Garside helped his son up, and whilst Vernon gathered the reins of their horses, Martin and his father walked the few hundred yards to the ranch.

On the way there, they passed the body of the man Durant had slain.

'I don't know him,' drawled Garside. 'He must have been one of the new men that Steve—'

He stopped short. Gunshots exploded at the ranch.

'God alive,' roared Durant. 'Hell's broke loose!'

They were out. Steve plunged into the dark yard his pistol blazing, fire ripping off the muzzle's end as slugs erupted toward the posted guard of a few men. Close by, Harry and Dane Chandler blasted away in unison, Harry cocking and firing his gun as quick as he could, each blast drilling lead toward the out-buildings.

Muzzle roars barked back – slugs slamming into the ranch house walls or biting into the baked earth of the yard. Despite his injured arm, Steve dived off his feet, rolling to his left and coming up again on one knee. Harry and Dane, bolting to the right, kept up a fierce shot rate and Steve waited for one of the enemy to fire again. When a spark of flame heralded a muzzle blast by the barn door, Steve dispatched a bullet right at it. A second later, laughter confirmed he'd missed his man.

'Goddamn,' Steve raged. 'I'll get you yet, scum.'

The other loyal ranch-hands showed then, Claude Lloyd blasting a carbine as the others drilled pistol bullets in the direction of the enemy.

Then things turned bad. They took hits – two of the loyal men crashing to ground, one struck in the guts, the other slain instantly by a bullet to the head.

They charged in a line toward the outbuildings, their barrage of fire relentless and scything into the wood walls of the outbuildings ahead. Yet, still the answering gun blasts came, firearms cracking out their answers in missiles of lead. A third of their men crumpled to his knees clutching at his stomach.

'Get back,' cried Harry Turner. 'Get back to the house.'

They began to retreat, hurtling toward the ranch house with weaving runs when a loud clamour signalled the arrival of others.

They rode in like a thunderous apocalypse – mounted men blasting their guns in blazing, bloody retribution.

Steve watched aghast as that silver-haired drifter who'd winged him a couple of days before charged his mustang across the yard, a Colt to hand and dispatched an inch perfect shot into the throat of one of Riley's men. Next, two other mounted men shot another off his feet. Silver-hair reined round and drove in again. A further gun blast sent a slug into the midriff of the last High S assailant.

When the gun sounds had faded to silence, Steve and the others inched forward. The battle was over. In a yard reeking of smoke and cordite, a heck of a lot of men lay dead.

Durant jumped off his mustang and approached Steve Doughty.

'We meet again, feller.'

Steve nodded, lifting his injured arm. 'I still feel it.'

'We lost three good men as well,' returned Steve. 'Our man Saul's missing too.'

'We need to talk,' drawled Durant.

Harry Turner, enraged, tried to mount up and ride straight for Cooper's Town.

Durant gripped his arm with a restraining hand. 'Don't be a fool. There're enough of them still out there.'

'But my wife,' raged Harry. 'I need to get back.'

'Don't worry,' returned Durant. 'We got to check on young Martin first.'

'I got to get there,' screamed Harry, fighting as Claude and Dane held him back now. 'You don't understand!'

'I reckon I do,' intoned Durant. 'You're not the only one with something to lose in Cooper's Town.'

CHAPTER SIXTEEN

Becky wept steadily as both Anne and Clara com-
forted her. Mayor Lassiter hung by the door of the
Carling shack, anxious to ride out with the posse but
wanting to be there in his official capacity when
Becky learnt the tragic news. He lowered his head,
feeling the young woman's pain.

'He weren't the best husband of late,' sobbed
Becky. 'But something changed him. Now his child's
to grow up without a pa.'

Anne didn't know what to say, despite the fact that
losing a husband she could sympathize with – and
one with a fault.

'We'll stay with you, Becky,' she reassured, 'for a
while yet at least.'

Clara clutched the bereaved woman's hand whilst
Anne moved across to speak to Lassiter. They
stepped out on to the boardwalk.

'We best ride out to the High S,' said the mayor.
'There's no telling what we'll find.'

'And John?' said Anne, struggling to keep her

voice steady. 'You'll look for him?'

'Once we've dealt with the High S,' said Lassiter. 'We'll set straight for Franklin's Forest.'

'Something has to be wrong,' Anne snapped. 'He should have been back by now.'

'Finding Vernon in a forest that size at night could take time, Anne,' said Lassiter. 'There's our sheriff too.'

'Ex-sheriff,' barked Anne. 'I'll take his badge off myself.'

Lassiter nodded. He turned but then halted. 'You don't suppose—'

'What?'

Lassiter shrugged. 'Oh, it's nothing. It was just a fancy of mine.' He doffed his hat and strode down the street.

'Mayor Lassiter?'

He stopped and looked back. 'Yes, Mrs Slocum.'

'I'll ask him to stay. That's what I'd like very much.'

'Yeah,' drawled the mayor, 'We'd all want that!'

'Riley did all the negotiations with those smallholders,' said Steve as they drank whiskey in the ranch house reception room. 'He'd tell me how much each farmer wanted, I'd give him the money and he'd come back with the signed deeds.' Steve laid his glass aside. 'I knew there'd been difficulty with the feller at Green Ash; he was the last to sell up.'

Steve lifted the pile of papers Harry had retrieved from the safe in the office. He sifted through them and produced the deed for Green Ash Farm. He passed it to Durant. 'Look, it's been duly signed.'

Durant looked confused. 'Don't it need to be done in front of a lawyer or a banker or some such?'

'Out here,' said Steve, 'No it don't. We operate a bit different, Mr Durant. So long as a recognized official witnesses the exchange then it's all legal.'

Durant sighed, instinctively knowing the answer to the question he was about to ask.

'Tell me,' he said sombrely. 'Who can witness?'

Steve shrugged. 'Mayor Lassiter and—' Steve stopped short and shook his head.

'Don't tell me,' growled Durant, 'Sheriff Makin?'

'That's about the size of it.' Steve put the papers aside. 'I've been stupid, Mr Durant. Taking on the High S went to my head and I took on the wrong sort. I heaped a heck of trouble on too many folk. I'm right sorry and got to make that up somehow.'

'A fool you might have been,' drawled Durant. 'But you didn't kill anybody; from what I've seen only Makin and Riley Saunders have done that.'

Steve nodded. 'I'm sorry about your friend Luke Gray.'

'I'll pay my respects when the time's right,' returned Durant. 'Right now we got to head to Cooper's Town to take down Saunders and his men. You say Makin's with them.'

'Not by choice,' offered Dane Chandler. 'Riley gave Makin a bit of a beating from the sound of it.'

'And Riley said Makin cut Luke Gray?'

Steve nodded. 'We all heard that.'

Harry had been pacing the hall and he darted into the room.

'Hell,' he spat. 'We gonna sit all night jawing or go save my wife from those scum?'

'We go now,' said Durant climbing to his feet. He glanced at Steve. 'You'll stay here with your men to secure the ranch.'

'No!' barked Steve. 'I already said I've got to make amends. I want to be there when Riley's taken down.'

Harry shrugged. 'I reckon he should go.'

Ten minutes later, six of them – Durant, Garside and his son Wade, Vernon, Harry Turner and Steve Doughty – galloped out of the High S yard toward the prairie. They left Martin at the ranch house where Dane Chandler tended to the wound. Claude Lloyd supervised the cleaning up. Sombrely, the loyal Doughty men began to gather up the bodies.

They'd devoured the distance to Cooper's Town and now held their mounts in a line several hundred feet beyond the settlement's western edge. They could see the yellow of lamps on the boardwalk posts and glowing through windows; they also observed the activity of men and horses where the thoroughfare gave out to the flatland grass.

'Looks like a posse's got up,' said Clem.

'Hell,' spat Makin despite his mounting terror. 'They wouldn't do squat when I asked them before.'

'That's justice for you,' laughed Riley. 'You could-n't rouse a posse but now those very men are set to

137

hunt you down.' Riley spat at the underfoot of parched prairie. 'They'll have a heck of rawhide I shouldn't wonder.'

Makin gulped, the thought of his perilous situation turning his guts and making him tremble. The enormity of his situation had struck home. Held as he was now by Riley and his cohorts, he faced either a knife-cut end at the hands of the psychopath or a lynch mob of Cooper's Town residents. He cursed his misfortune. Durant had caused it all. If that silver-hair hadn't showed, things would have been as always. The ex-federal had destroyed the sheriff's life and if the opportunity arose, Makin would slay Durant by any means possible.

'When we get into town,' said Riley to Makin, 'You take us to Turner's wife and this skirt Durant's been sniffing about.'

Makin replied with a nod.

'Right,' growled Riley. 'We go in fast and shooting before that posse gets mounted up.'

A moment later, with terrifying howls and raking spurs to their mounts, Riley and his crew plunged toward Cooper's Town. They hit the town fast, their guns blasting.

To those on Main Street's boardwalks it sounded like hell itself had just ridden in.

Mayor Lassiter checked his six-shooter, slid it into the holster on his right hip and had his foot in the stirrup of his pinto mare when the blasts began. He lurched back and grabbed for his gun. He threw a frantic glance towards the prairie and watched in horror as a mass of mounted men, their guns spewing flame, thundered into town.

A man on the boardwalk, spinning pathetically as a slug struck, uttered a guttural cry and crashed over the rail to land grotesquely on the thoroughfare's rutted surface.

Men scattered down the street, their startled horses screaming and bolting in all directions. Now all sought cover and a firing position. A local sprinted for a rain barrel but died before he got there. Taking a bullet in the back, he slammed to his knees before keeling over to bleed his last in the dust.

Lassiter drew his gun and got off a shot. The pistol shuddered in his grip as the slug departed and one of the riders clutched desperately at his face as a bullet ripped into his left eye. A second later, wailing with agony, the mortally wounded man departed the back of his horse and hit the street's surface with a grunt of death.

Now Lassiter ran for his life. Panic gripped him as he flew down an alleyway. His wife – alone now upstairs at the hardware – would be terrified but he couldn't reach her. He darted down the dark passage and tried to think straight. He had to find some-where to hide and pray none of those riders came after him. He threw himself into the black shadows and crossed street after street.

At last, he slowed and took his bearings. Panting, his heart pumping fit to burst and his lungs and legs aching, he looked around. He stumbled toward Becky Carling's shack. He'd hole up in there until this horror was over.

Riley dismounted and hitched his horse to the rail outside the Stage Saloon. His men soon did likewise and they all surveyed the bodies strewn along Main Street.

'Al's bought it,' growled Clem Daly.

Riley nodded. 'We got a couple of theirs.' He kicked at the corpse of the man blasted clean over the boardwalk's side rail. He spat at it with the curse, 'Goddamn piece of scum.'

'It's someone's pa or husband,' returned Tom Leyton.

Riley jerked out his knife and jabbed it at the red-haired younger man. Tom staggered back and Riley laughed raucously.

'You're right twitchy ain't you, Tommy?'

'Hell's teeth,' spat Leyton. 'I'd wish you'd lay off with that knife, Riley. It makes me nervous.'

Riley slid the knife back in his belt and pointed at the Stage. 'We'll wash the dust with Bert and then think some.' He spun round and grabbed for Sheriff Makin who stood isolated and trembling nearby. 'You're coming with us, dirt ball.' He shoved Makin up the boardwalk steps.

'Please,' Makin whined. 'We got to split from town fast. We'll all swing for what's gone on.'

Makin had got to the top of the steps now and tried to resist the push toward the saloon. Another of

Riley's crew darted forward and put out a restraining arm.

'Hell, Riley, we missed a trick there. This crooked law's still got his Colt strapped on. He could have blasted any of us out on the ride here.' He slid his hand across and drew the Peacemaker out of Makin's holster. 'You won't need this iron again.'

Riley sighed. 'I'm getting too trusting in my old age.'

'Nice gun this,' drawled the one with the Peacemaker. He backed away towards the batwings waving the pistol in his hand. 'I might even use it, instead of mine.'

His back touched the batwings and he eased in. 'Come on, boys, let's get us some redeye.'

A sickening boom erupted from within the saloon and the man at the batwings flew forward again, his body decimated by the fired contents of Bert Lewis's 12 bore. Screaming to the last, the struck man, his back ripped apart, staggered down the boardwalk steps and crashed face down in the street. He groaned once, twitched sickeningly and then died.

The rest of the crew drove the saloon doors. Riley entered firing like a man possessed. A dozen slugs dispatched across the bar space until it was certain the risk had been eliminated.

A short while later – all of them inside the saloon now – they studied the slain body of the barkeep Bert Lewis. He lay dead, the wounds of many bullets to his front, a trickle of blood running from the left side of his mouth and painting his chin. His eyes were wide

141

and utterly still.

'Goddamn,' barked Riley spitting at the body. 'And I thought he liked us.'

'You just can't trust no one,' snarled Clem. He grabbed for a bottle of whiskey off the bar and made for the raised section. Others did the same and before long they all swallowed the fiery liquid with abandon. Makin cowered nearby, pressing back against a wall. He just stayed quiet, his look one of mortal sickness.

'That's some better,' gasped Riley at length. He removed a bottle from his lips. 'It burns good and that's no mistake.'

'Say, Riley,' returned Clem. 'I reckon Makin's right. The whole darn shooting match is blown. We should cut dirt and get out of this place.'

'We will,' intoned Riley. 'First I want some fun with two little gals. I need me a going away present and I reckon they'll be just plumb perfect.'

CHAPTER SEVENTEEN

A rapping on the shack door made them all scream. They clutched at each other, a collective panic gripping the room. At length, when the rapping persisted, Anne climbed shakily to her feet.

She listened intently and heard a familiar voice. She threw open the door and Lassiter fell in.

'Hell,' hissed the mayor. 'Praise you're all still here.'

Anne slammed and locked the door and then clutched at the town official. 'What's happened?' she wailed. 'I mean – all that shooting!'

'Riley Saunders,' returned Lassiter sinking on to a chair. 'He and a load of his boys have killed a few fellers in Main Street.' Lassiter shook his head. 'That last lot of gun blasting might mean more are dead.'

'I've got to get home,' responded Anne with trembling words. 'Pa will be worried sick.'

Lassiter looked a man drained – all the colour

sucked from his face whilst his eyes were wide and telling of some inner anguish.

'Seems we're on our own,' he mumbled. 'Durant won't—'

'He'll be here,' barked Anne. 'I just know it. We've got to hide up till John returns. He'll know what to do.'

Lassiter nodded. 'OK, Annie. But hell, hide where?'

Anne sighed. 'I'll get Pa and show you. We've got to go.'

Together they exited the shack – three women, one baby and the mayor. All of them terrified and keeping to the shadows of the street's edge, they scurried on toward the Slocum home.

They drove on toward Cooper's Town, the only noise the drumming intensity of their mounts' massed hoofs.

Only once, a while back, had someone spoken.

'Please,' Harry bellowed out. 'Please let us be in time.'

Now, as he rode, Durant's mind raged with intense thoughts. He ached for his dead wife but she was gone. That life finished with, he needed a new way. In the tragedy of his wife's demise and seeking and losing Luke he'd found something – no, someone – who would spark his life with purpose again. Anne! He knew he loved and needed her. Afterwards, when all returned to order, he'd hold her in his arms again and utter the words he hoped she'd want to hear.

144

Would she agree to marry him, though? He dismissed this and longed for her.

He recalled that last meeting with the Head of the US Marshal's office in Morton.

You've got trigger-hnappy, Durant. If trouble hits I'm not so sure you'd be clear-headed enough to take the right men down. Grief can do that to a feller. It can make him hate everything and everyone in the whole goddamn world.

Durant shook that memory out of his mind. He dug his spurs in and drove the mustang on.

'Come on, boy,' he muttered to the horse as the dark miles flew by. 'I hope Emma would understand. Love can do stuff to a feller too. . . . I don't hate the goddamn world – just the scum that's on it.'

Riley descended the boardwalk steps and surveyed their handiwork. The bodies of the Cooper's Town men still lay where they'd fallen – grotesque testament to public duty gone wrong. Clem, Tom Leyton and the remainder of the crew bunched in the street. Makin stood close by, a pistol's muzzle trained on him.

Riley shook his head. 'Goddamn,' he spat. 'Months of work and it's all lost.'

'We got to go,' drawled Clem. 'It won't be long till the deputy shows; we just don't know who he'll bring with him.'

Riley scowled. 'I came to do summat and that's

what I'm gonna do.' He nodded at Clem. 'Leave two fellers here to warn if anyone comes near. Rest of you follow me.' He stepped forward and grabbed Makin roughly by the shirt. 'Where's Turner's place?'

Five minutes later, finding the Turner residence locked and in darkness, Riley smashed out a window and clambered in. Others followed and a rapid search confirmed the building to be empty. Exiting, Makin led them through the alleys into Liberty Street. Men dispersed, some to check the shack Durant rented and others to search the Slocum home.

'They've all gone,' confirmed Clem.

Riley scanned down the street. All the houses and shacks sat in silent blackness and he suspected people hid inside, each praying for salvation. His eyes alighted then on the tall, dilapidated form of the Bellfield Hotel. He jabbed the muzzle of his gun at it. He recalled then that Old Ned Slocum owned it and that the hotel went out of business when the passenger stage stopped pulling through.

He stepped closer and bellowed loudly, 'We can't find Harry Turner's woman or the Slocum gal. Unless we see them soon I reckon we'll start searching house by house. Any young un's we find we'll kill!'

Stillness held and Riley sent a slug skyward with an echoing bang.

'I'm not messing,' he roared as the gun blast subsided. 'Now boys, get ready to slaughter any kid you see.'

A door on to the balcony opened and Anne stepped out.

'Animal,' she screamed. 'What d'you want of me and Clara?'

'Oh,' drawled Riley. 'Just my dues.'

Anne shook her head. 'Haven't you done enough damage? God alive, John Durant's headed here and he'll catch you and you'll all swing.'

'I don't have much time then,' returned Riley. 'So you and Clara Turner get your hides here fast and we'll get it done.'

Anne gave a sob and shouted, 'Wait there; we'll be down.'

She stepped into the dank hotel bedroom where they'd all crowded.

'You can't go out there,' exclaimed Lassiter. 'They might—'

'I know exactly what they'll do,' returned Anne. 'If I don't submit you heard they'd slaughter every child they find.'

Old Ned's eyes filled. 'I won't permit it, Annie, gal. I'll sooner die myself.'

Anne shook her head and stepped forward to hug her elderly father. 'Hush, Pa, it'll soon be done with.'

Clara rose from a seat and sighed. 'I'm ready too.'

They descended the unlit stairway, groping their way across the foyer to the front door. A turn of the key saw them outside, both trembling on the board-walk.

Riley approached and chuckled. He grabbed Anne by her hair and dragged her across the street.

Throwing her through the doorway of the home she shared with her father, he followed and forced her into one of the bedrooms.

He put his revolver aside and began to unbuckle his belt. 'Get yourself ready,' he drawled. 'I'll give you summat to remember me by!'

They reined up at the edge of town, each of their mounts snorting its exhaustion. They'd crossed the distance at a pace no man would call reasonable but thankfully their animals had held up. They'd had to risk it. Now, with only a couple of boardwalk lamps casting any light in the settlement, Durant pondered on what to do.

He glanced sideways and saw a clump of trees. 'We'll hitch the horses here and go in on foot.'

This soon done, they inched forward. A hundred yards or so from Main Street's edge Durant sighted a guard. He dropped to ground and others followed rapidly.

They waited then, watching intently to see another pacing close by.

'Just the two hawks,' hissed Harry. 'We can take 'em both out, no worry.'

'Knives!' whispered Durant. 'I don't want Saunders to get warning we're here.'

They moved on, stopping again mere feet from the two grumbling men slouched against the board-walk rail. Durant thrust his Colt at Vernon and slid a knife out of his belt. Harry hauled his own pistol up and clutched the butt tightly.

Steve moved forward then, his knife already to hand. He tapped Durant's arm. 'Come on, let's do it.'

The two men made soft steps to a place where they could launch an attack. Those guards, still idly leaning against the rail, didn't know what hit them. Both Durant and Steve hurtled forward together, Durant smashing in to one and knocking him off his feet. The guard's rifle spilled from his grasp and as he struggled to regain his feet and grab for the gun, Durant plunged his knife's blade into the man's back. A pathetic cry and gasp ensued before the hoodlum perished.

Steve, though, struggled. He'd shoulder-barged his man but that guard hadn't fallen. He staggered back a few feet, his rifle thrown from his grasp, but he regained composure quickly and had a Colt to hand.

He aimed it at the startled Steve. 'Well, boy, this is where it ends.'

'Go to hell, Levi Brakes,' spat the young ranch boss.

Levi grinned and levelled his arm to fire.

Steve jabbed the knife. 'I'll cut you, Levi.'

Levi laughed. 'Give it a rest, boy.'

Steve stood up straight and gave a sigh. 'I reckon you've done for me.'

Levi looked confused. He hesitated, unable to fathom a man just accepting his fate like this.

A split second offered enough. Steve, gripping the knife blade between thumb and forefinger propelled it with ruthless speed. It span the distance with a barely audible whistle before the blade end impaled, with sickening perfection, in Levi's throat. Brakes dropped his gun, clutched at his neck and then slumped to the earth where the blood seeped out of him.

Steve gaped at Levi's outstretched form, beset by twitches until the stillness of death settled in.

Durant stepped forward and extracted the knife. 'Damn good hit, kid.'

He passed the knife back but Steve just let it fall. He hauled his pistol out of its holster.

The others had joined them now.

'Right,' said Durant. 'We go forward carefully. We'll check the saloon then your house, Harry.'

Turner nodded.

They spanned the width of Main Street, men armed and determined. If they had their way, the only ending on this bloody night would be one of revenge and justice.

CHAPTER EIGHTEEN

Anne listened to Clara's screams from the other bedroom.

A man's voice sounded then: harsh, cruel, demanding.

'Bitch,' he bellowed. 'Stop fighting it. You're gonna do what I say.'

'Bastard,' screamed Clara. 'I'll die first.' The sound of crashing glass sounded and Riley chuckled.

'Hell,' he muttered. 'She's a feisty one, ain't she?' He glared leeringly at Anne. 'You ready, whore? You best get your dress off.'

Anne shook her head and feinted to lift her clothing.

'I won't struggle,' she muttered. 'Just get it done with.'

Riley grinned and dropped his gunbelt.

Anne launched herself then. She hurtled forward, slamming into Riley with one of her shoulders and driving him off his feet. He howled, stumbling back and crashing to the floor. A second later, he lurched upright again and cursed loudly.

Anne scrambled over to Riley's gunbelt. She got to it, her shaking hands frantically dragging the pistol from its holster. Now, the gun to hand, she jabbed the muzzle at this sneering nemesis.

'You goddamn beast,' she cried. 'I'll blast you to hell.'

He held there half-dressed and unsure. 'Now, missy, put that gun down before you hurt yourself.'

She jabbed the pistol, her eyes wide and hate surging through her. Her finger tensed at the trigger.

'So help me,' she screamed. 'I'll—' She stopped short, another prolonged scream from Clara turning her blood cold.

She plunged out of the room and along the corridor. Soon, driving at the door of the other bedroom – that place where Clara suffered – she viewed the startled eyes of a man who held a clenched fist over Clara's bruised form.

'Die, pig,' Anne howled. The gun jumped in her hand and the muzzle exploded with flame and smoke. An instant later, a slug slamming into his stomach, the man spun and slammed into the wall. He held there a moment, before sliding down to lie in a spreading pool of blood.

Anne burst into tears and ran to Clara. They clung to each other and prayed.

The gun blast had them running. They made the corner of Liberty Street at a sprint and when Durant saw men outside the Slocum house, his guts lurched.

'Anne,' he yelled, grabbing his Colt off Vernon and tearing forward.

Amongst the outlaws, Clem, Tom and one of their other crew waited with Makin on the street. Clem had half moved toward the house when the gun blast sounded, but the noise of running footfalls caught all their attention.

Tom lunged for his gun but Durant had already fired. A slug ripped into Leyton's head, brains spraying out in a shower of blood before the body dropped useless and past life into the dust.

Clem reached his pistol and got a shot off. The bullet departed and slammed into Wade Garside's thigh. The young man cried out in agony and slumped to his knees before keeling face-down on to the street.

Harry didn't hesitate. He took aim and drilled lead into Clem's guts. Riley's right-hand man staggered back clutching his midriff. A moment later, with an agonized wail, Clem collapsed onto his back.

The last of Riley's crew had run. He belted down Liberty Street with Steve Doughty in pursuit. Steve, a pistol to hand now, stopped suddenly and took aim. The fleeing hoodlum had almost reached the street's end when Steve compressed the trigger. His gun's muzzle barked out that fatal message. The man fell, a bullet to the small of his back. He'd died before he met the dry, baked earth below.

Makin hadn't moved. He held there, frozen, arms aloft.

Garside covered the sheriff while Durant plunged

into the Slocum house. He tore through the front room and into the nearest bedroom. He stopped short and studied the scene.

Anne and Clara held on to each other beside the bed. Behind it, a dead man still bled. Riley Saunders, his gun recovered from where Anne had hurled it, had the revolver trained on the two women.

'Hell's teeth,' spat Riley. 'That bitch you fancy gets my gun, kills my man, then she throws this piece aside. You couldn't reckon it.'

Anne began to weep. 'John,' she sobbed. 'I'm sorry. I was that scared I didn't think straight.'

Riley waggled his revolver at Anne and Clara. 'Drop that piece, silver-hair.'

Durant cast the Colt out of the room.

'They're both innocent in all this, Saunders.'

Riley laughed. 'Hell, Durant, it don't mean nothing to me. Guilty or innocent – it's just the same if they get in my way.'

He levelled the pistol and twitched his finger at the trigger. 'Your bit of skirt – she didn't do what I wanted!'

A sudden crash sounded and the window imploded, shattered glass spraying across the room. Riley's attention taken for a moment, Durant hurtled forwards. He threw himself across the room, slamming a fist to the side of Riley's head, then grabbing desperately for the other's gun.

Riley bellowed in rage and, retaining his hold on the pistol, slammed his finger to the trigger. The gun jerked and blasted its slug, but, off balance now,

Riley's shot flew left and slammed into the wall.

Anne and Clara screamed hysterically, but seeing their chance of escape they both rushed for the door.

Riley and Durant fought on. They struggled across the room, Riley straining to angle his gun's muzzle into Durant's chest. They locked out to standstill.

'I'll not stop,' panted Riley. 'You'll weaken before I do.'

'Go to hell,' gasped Durant, his arms aching with the struggle to resist the force of the other.

Still they both held, their respective bodyweight counterbalancing the strain of the other.

Finally, Durant's rugged 200lbs enduring, Riley began to weaken. Durant saw it in Saunders' eyes. The outlaw blinked and his eyes widened. Finally, his arms began to sag and Durant forced him down to his knees and extricated the gun from his grip. He dragged Riley up with the pistol's muzzle pressed to the outlaw's temple.

'You're under arrest,' sighed Durant. 'For just about everything, I'd reckon.'

He dragged Riley out into the street where Harry trained his gun on the outlaw. Garside Senior tended to Wade, who, in pain but alive, raised an arm to signify his wellbeing.

Anne flew at Durant, embracing him as if she never wanted to let go. Clara appeared then, running to her husband and hugging him tightly.

'Woman,' muttered Harry. 'I thought I'd die getting here.'

'But you did get here,' she said. 'And I'm never

155

letting you out my sight again.'

Old Ned, Lassiter and Becky Carling clutching the baby exited the hotel and soon other town folk began to gravitate there.

Durant locked Anne with a passionate, lingering kiss.

He broke from this briefly, to call out, 'It's OK; it's all over now.'

Anne drew her lips back to his. Nothing else existed then except the unfathomable notion that the whole world was clapping.

Two weeks passed before Judge Alfred Addison hit Cooper's Town. Others came: Marshal Leon Lines from Nebraska replete with a saddle-bag of greenback bills for the slaying of Clem Daly and Tom Leyton. A small fortune came for the capture of Riley Saunders. Added to the amounts for the minor members of Riley's crew it constituted a pretty sum.

It went to quick and good use. Anne and her father set to re-opening the Bellfield Hotel. Many people helped and it now gleamed resplendent with a lick of new paint and fully renovated inside.

Two deputies had volunteered and been hired. Durant, offered the sheriff's position, had accepted without reservation. When the business with Riley and Makin concluded, he needed a period of leave to return to Morton to sell his home and tie up loose ends there.

The trial lasted three days. An open and shut case as they say. The verdicts: Riley Saunders found guilty of multiple murders and a catalogue of other crimes; ex-sheriff Blair Makin found guilty of the murders of Frank Carling and Lyle Malone. The court also found Makin – by a unanimous margin – guilty of torturing Luke Gray. Both men spent their tenure in the Cooper's Town jail in adjacent cells and cursing each other each dawn until dusk.

Now, on this day, as a warm sun baked the vast grassland terrain and the town resounded to hammering as the gallows went up in Main Street, Anne and Durant took a buggy out to Franklin's Forest. Vernon led on a horse. They brought flowers that Durant laid at the gravesite of his oldest friend.

They rode back then, Durant flicking at the reins. Halfway there, a mass of mounted men approached fast from the west and Durant smiled.

'Howdy, Sheriff,' called out Steve. 'Mind if we accompany you into town?'

Durant doffed his hat. 'Be my guest.'

'I'm selling the farms,' said Steve as he let his horse amble beside the buggy. 'About Green Ash, I just wondered—'

Durant shook his head. 'Sell to good people; Luke would be happy with that.'

'Harry,' said Steve then. 'He's set to retire.'

'Yeah,' returned Durant. 'He will be missed, I'd reckon.'

'True,' Steve drawled. 'He's taught me a lot.'

'Your pa would be proud,' offered Anne. 'You made mistakes but learnt from them.'

Steve nodded. 'I'll make the High S what it was. I

won't lose what Pa built for me.'

They saw Cooper's Town now – rising out of the dry prairie. The whole populace thronged the main thoroughfare to see justice done. Judge Addison and Marshal Lines presided over the executions and a man especially brought in from Missouri settled the ropes over the necks of the condemned.

Riley ascended the steps to the decking with bravado and a circumspect attitude.

'It'll be a rough reception t'other side,' he drawled. 'Goddamn it, I've sent enough dogs there before me.'

Three men had to drag a screaming and crying Makin up there. He sobbed as the rope addressed the skin of his neck.

'Let me go,' he howled. 'It ain't my fault. I don't want to die.'

Anne gasped as the executioner strode to the lever.

Makin continued to sob, but Riley, defiant, cursed them all. At last, his invective spent, he sighed, 'Why did I come to such a dirt-pile piece of country as this?' He sneered at Durant. 'You, silver-hair, why do you stay in this godforsaken place?'

Durant gripped Anne's hand and said, 'For good people and a beautiful woman.'

She leant across and they kissed.

Riley nodded. 'Ah well, a right cosy arrangement?' He turned his head and snapped at Makin, 'Goddamn it, stop that snivelling and take it like a man.'

The executioner began to draw back on the mechanism.

'I don't want to die,' screamed Makin. 'Why should I? What is my death for—'

The lever went with a thunderous crash, both bodies dropping like stones through the open traps.

Anne looked away and a gasp went up. Then silence prevailed.

Durant watched the corpses sway to stillness. People began to disperse. A while later, as he led Anne toward Liberty Row, the only sounds of that still hot, late afternoon were the rumbling approach of the first stagecoach for months and the bellowed cries of the departing Steve Doughty and his loyal hands.

Their words rang long in Durant's memory – as if answering Makin's plaintive pleading whilst carrying back to the very land itself. It seemed to echo for miles.

'That's for hell and the High S!'